Guilty Kisses

Killarney Sheffield

MuseItUp Publishing
www.museituppublishing.com

MuseItUp Publishing
14878 James, Pierrefonds, Quebec, Canada, H9H 1P5
http://www.museituppublishing.com

Cover Art © 2010 by Delilah K. Stephens
Edited by Nancy Bell
Copyedited by Greta Gunselman
Layout and Book Production by Lea Schizas

Print ISBN: 978-1-927085-11-0
eBook ISBN: 978-1-926931-81-4
First eBook Edition * June 2011
Production by MuseItUp Publishing

GUILTY KISSES

BY

KILLARNEY SHEFFIELD

Dedication

To Lea Schizas who had faith in me, and to my family who never said I couldn't do it. Thanks isn't enough.

Acknowledgements

Thanks to Sharon Lauermilk and Teresa L. Hamlin whose book, "The Regency Companion," is my writing bible.

Chapter One

This should be the happiest day of her seventeen years. Cassie turned full circle in front of the mirror. Why didn't she follow her heart and run away while she had a chance? It was too late now and would only bring shame and hardship on her family. She brushed away a golden curl escaping from its artful arrangement; already a few wisps framed her pale face. The blue eyes staring back at her were unusually flat and emotionless, while a delicate frown creased her forehead.

"Oh, you look so pretty!" Younger by a mere twelve months, her exuberant sister flounced into the room.

Cassie smiled at the reflection in the mirror. Beth was so similar in looks they were often mistaken for twins, except her sibling was much more confident.

"I am pea green with envy. You will be the centre of attention. I wish it was me."

"That makes two of us, Beth." Cassie smoothed the shiny blue satin skirt of her wedding dress to still her shaking hands.

The rustle of skirts announced her mother's entrance. "Oh, Cassandra, you are lovely. Lord Everton is going to adore you." Her blue eyes sparkled with unshed tears as she fussed with the tiny buttons on the back of the gown.

Cassie rolled her eyes, struggling to keep the bitterness from her voice. "Lord Everton does not seem the type to adore anything, let alone a bride he has only met once."

Her mother's stern look quelled her rebellion. "Cassandra, we have been over this, Lord Everton is a better match than we could have ever hoped for. Just think, you will be the wife of an earl. You must agree it is better than marrying a commoner. Just think of the lovely things he will give you, not to mention all the servants. You will never want for anything."

Cassie sighed. "I know. I just wish he was not quite so...old."

Beth handed her a bright bouquet of fall leaves. "He is not that old."

"Beth! He is sixty-years-old if he's a day, and has outlasted three wives." Exasperation tinged her voice, fueled by her sister's constant attempts to see the good in everything.

Her mother smiled, carefully placing a matching wreath of leaves on her head and pinning it in place. "So he is experienced." She blushed and leaned closer. "It is good he is experienced in the marriage bed, he will be gentle and considerate of your innocence."

"Mamma!" the girls cried in mortified unison.

She gave them a wry smile and shook her head. "Come on, you have kept the earl waiting long enough."

Cassie took one last look in the mirror. Would she appear the same on the morrow or did getting married change one somehow? She could not see anything changing except her status and home. Loathing filled her at the thought of marrying an older man who she knew so little about. Hopefully the earl was a different man than his first impression implied. Mayhap he really was kind, gentle, and romantic. It was possible she misjudged him, she thought, following her mother and sister into the corridor.

Her father approached to escort her to the chapel where he would officiate the marriage. Cassie returned his smile with a tight one of her own. Morning light accentuated the shine of her father's bald pate ringed with a wispy fringe of grey hair. His normally merry eyes were barren of emotion. How strange she never noticed how frail he was until today. She would miss helping him with his sermons and book work.

She was doing the right thing. She tried to convince herself, even though she had no say in the matter. The money the earl promised upon her conception of an heir would help ease her father's burden. It was a poor parish with many to feed, and their own large family placed a huge strain on him.

Her gaze focused on her elderly husband-to-be waiting at the pulpit. Earl Everton leaned heavily on his cane and offered a distorted smile, his lips curling up on one side but sagging on the other. She suppressed a small shudder. No doubt the stroke the earl suffered the previous year accounted for his strange leer.

She looked down at her feet, the tips of her mother's marriage slippers poking out from under the hem of her borrowed gown. Gathering her courage, she forced her unwilling feet to bring her to the earl's side. Her father placed her hand in the earl's cold one; the man's grip was frail and his skin papery. Cassie suppressed another shudder and cast a shy glance at her future husband.

The earl turned to listen to her father as he blessed their union, and Cassie concentrated on the ceremony rather than his raspy breathing. This was supposed to be a joyous day, but all she could feel was dread. What could she possibly have to talk to the earl about? Surely any of her interests would seem silly and childish to him. Cassie sighed. There was nothing to do but make the best of the situation. She stared blankly at the floor, afraid to look at her father lest she break down and cry.

Before she knew it the ceremony was over. A footman brought her new pastel blue cloak and assisted her with it. Numbly she descended the steps and allowed him to hand her into the earl's luxurious carriage. Cassie sent a silent goodbye to her former life as the carriage door slammed shut behind the earl.

She stared out the window as the carriage started forward. People were filing from the church and making their way to their own conveyances. A large luncheon at her new home was planned to celebrate their wedding. It was a relief to know it would be hours before she must face her first night in a marriage bed.

Resigned to her fate, Cassie watched the scenery, her breath fogging up the glass. A few snowflakes drifted upon the crisp fall breeze, signaling the impending approach of winter's wiles. Ignoring her dozing husband, she watched as the carriage wound through the streets of London. Small houses gave way to small shops, and then to larger houses. Finally the opulent mansions of the wealthy commanded her attention. One of these great houses was now her home. The horses pulled up in front of a mansion, the red brick walls cheery against the grey of the fall day. Great sandstone pillars flanked the steps which led to the massive double doors. She refused to let the size daunt her since everything today was bigger than life.

Cassie waited for the footman to come around and set out the foot stool. After he helped her husband alight he held out his hand to her.

She smiled her thanks and descended. The young man's face remained expressionless when he placed her hand on the old man's arm. Cassie took a deep breath, raised her chin, and accompanied the earl up the stone steps. A butler hurried forward to open the doors and receive their wraps.

She gasped. Her family's cozy four bedroom cottage could fit inside the foyer of this grand place. Her home now, she corrected herself. Their footsteps echoed as they crossed the earth-colored tiles, following the servant toward a large set of open doors. The earl led Cassie into a cavernous formal dining room with the longest table she had ever seen. She counted the dinner services as they moved to their places at the head of the table. *Forty! Good Lord! Is this what the earl considers an informal dinner party?*

Earl Everton cleared his throat. "Ahem."

Cassie looked up. He favored her with an impatient look and indicated she should sit in the chair a footman held waiting for her. She settled herself and looked down at the lace table cloth. A gold-edged plate, a silver dinner service, a crystal wine glass, and a delicate monogrammed napkin decorated each place setting. Spots swam before her eyes at the sight. *What if I use the wrong fork? What if I knock over one of the delicate wine glasses?* Everyone would guess how unused to wealth she was. She clutched the folds of her gown in her hands. It would be mortifying if she embarrassed the earl and her family.

Her husband took his seat at the head of the table as guests began to file into the room. Her despair increased, she shot her parents an uneasy look as they took their seats to her right. Once the guests were seated, a servant filled the wine glasses and the meal was served.

Cassie sipped the wine and pushed roast pheasant around her plate with the fork. A million butterflies fluttered within her stomach. She glanced around the room. Many ladies returned her look with curious ones of their own.

Heat flooded her cheeks as she recalled her first meeting with the earl two weeks earlier. He had inspected her as if she were a horse he wished to purchase until she feared she would expire from embarrassment. After proclaiming her of sturdy build, most promising for childbearing, he informed her parents he would take her to wife as soon as possible. If she conceived a child within the first year he promised to reward her father's small country parish with a large monetary donation. *Do the lords and ladies here tonight know of the arrangement? Perhaps not, and they wonder why an earl would marry a commoner like myself.*

Her mother cast an annoyed look in her direction and nodded to her plate.

Anger rose unbidden, pricking her already strained nerves. "I am not hungry."

"You should be honored to be seated at such a laden table. Many in our parish are in desperate need of such fare."

Cassie bowed her head. "Yes, Mamma."

She stabbed a piece of pheasant with her fork and lifted the morsel to her mouth. The tender meat, although perfectly cooked and seasoned, did nothing to tempt her absent appetite. She chewed and swallowed out of necessity. When the servant came to clear away her plate a few minutes later she was amazed to see it was half empty. The dinner sat like a rock in her stomach. The next course was served, and she pushed it away, directing a stubborn look in her mother's direction.

The afternoon dragged on as course after course was served. Never had she seen so much food. Finally the meal ended and everyone retired to the ballroom for the evening entertainments. Two hours passed while Cassie wistfully watched the couples dancing. Her husband had not bothered to ask her to dance yet and seemed unlikely to. She glanced at him out of the corner of her eye. He was talking to a group of men on the other side of the ballroom. She frowned. Except for her, everyone else was mingling and dancing, having a wonderful time.

A maid paused at her chair. "My lady, his lordship asked that I escort you and your mother to your chambers."

Cassie felt her stomach tighten. The dreaded hour was upon her. She stood. Her mother took her hand, and they followed the servant from the room. Cassie's legs threatened to buckle as they crossed the foyer and climbed the wide carpeted staircase to the second floor. The servant ushered them inside a bed chamber.

A large bed dominated the room, twice the size of the one she shared with Beth. It stood, raised on a platform, two feet off the ground. A set of narrow steps allowed the occupant easy access to the thick mattress. The room was decorated in creamy earthen colors similar to the grand foyer. A lively fire crackled in the hearth, adding warmth to the room. The thick oriental carpet muffled her footsteps as Cassie approached the fireplace, slipped between two chairs which flanked it, and held her hands out to the fire. They trembled despite the heat from the flames. *Will my husband come to my bed to consummate our marriage or will I be expected to go to him?*

Her mother led her to a tall ornate dressing screen in the corner. After helping Cassie with the row of tiny pearl buttons on the back of her wedding dress, she coaxed her behind the screen to undress. Cassie slid the cool silky dress down until it fell into a shimmering puddle at her feet. She stepped out of the circle of material and carefully laid it over the top of the screen. Her mother handed her a new sheer nightdress which she slipped over her head.

"Come now, child, it is time to brush out your hair."

Cassie emerged from behind the screen, crossing her arms over the revealing garment as embarrassment flooded her cheeks.

Her mother guided her to the dressing table beside a closed door and motioned for her to sit. "Are you nervous?"

Cassie regarded her mother's reflection in the mirror. She nodded, trying to enjoy the soothing brush strokes.

"There is nothing to be afraid of."

"What if I displease his lordship?"

"You cannot displease him if you do as he asks," her mother reassured her. "It will be over quickly, and it only hurts a little the first time. He will come often to your bed until you are with child after which he will not bother you with his needs until well after the birth. Pray you are breeding by Candle-mass and all will be well."

Cassie nodded, hiding her fear.

"I will leave you now." Cassie's mother put down the brush and pressed a quick kiss on top of her head. "You have always been a good and dutiful child. I wish you happiness. Goodbye, dear daughter."

Cassie stood uncertainly in the centre of the room; the sound of the door closing in her mother's wake filled her with the unaccustomed feeling of abandonment. Then she cried, stifling the overwhelming urge to fling open the bedroom door, run down the corridor, and beg her mother to come back. She crossed the room and sat in a chair by the fire. Pulling her feet up onto the seat, she wrapped her arms around her knees, and stared at the intimidating bed.

Perhaps she could bury herself so far down in the fluffy mattress the earl would not detect her presence in the gigantic bed. Mayhap he was poor of sight and would overlook her. She heaved a loud sigh. Both possibilities were doubtful. Her mind refused to come to grips with the idea the marriage bed was her lot in life. Tremors of apprehension coursed through her body. She shrank back into the cushion when the connecting door between the suites opened.

The earl hobbled into the room dressed in a long jonquil yellow silk robe and matching slippers. She choked back a nervous giggle; her new husband resembled a large Jamaican banana. Spying her huddled on the chair, he pinned her with an annoyed look. He crossed the room and shucked off his slippers, exposing a glimpse of his pale stick-like legs.

He gestured to the bed. "Come, girl, and do your duty."

Cassie blushed and moved woodenly to the bedside. Nervously she tried to postpone the inevitable. "I must say my prayers, my lord."

His brow furrowed with annoyance, but he nodded. "Get on with it then."

Cassie knelt by the side of the bed and closed her eyes. She clasped her shaking hands together in front of her and bowed her head. "Oh Lord, bless this day. Bless Mama and Papa. Watch over my sisters Beth, Ann, Ruth, and little Mary. Bless my brothers Nick, Paul, Mathew, Luke, and Baby John. Bless the poor and infirm. Look after the babies and children of our neighbors. I ask your guidance to help me be a good wife and lady. Please help me make Lord Everton happy and…Oh—"

"Amen," Lord Everton scowled.

"Amen," Cassie concluded. She climbed into the bed, pulled the covers up around her neck, and waited.

"First you must drink this special fertility potion." He held out a glass of brownish liquid.

Cassie took the glass and sniffed the contents. It smelled like the fishmonger's table at the market. When she glanced at him he nodded. Plugging her nose, she downed the foul-smelling concoction, gagging on its bitter taste. The earl nodded his approval, took the glass from her, and set it on the bedside table.

He leaned his cane against the table, and she closed her eyes, her body stiffening with dread. The mattress sagged as he climbed onto the bed beside her. With a grunt he flipped off the bedclothes and settled himself on top of her, groping between them and pulling her nightdress aside. Cassie held her breath as he fumbled. It took an extraordinarily long time before he pressed his manhood against her most private place. With a grunt he pushed forward. His rough entry forced a cry of pain from her lips. The earl ignored her and began to thrust frantically, grunting and panting. Cassie bit her lip as tears ran down her cheeks. *This is what a marriage bed entails? It is bestial and disgusting.*

He continued to rut until he uttered a long groan. Panting, he rolled off her. Cassie turned onto her side when he left, closing the door between their rooms, pulled the blankets over her head, and wept.

She poked her head from under the cover at the unexpected arrival of a maid. The girl motioned for Cassie to follow her through a door on the other side of the room. Inside was a large bathing tub. Hot water gurgled from the tap and splashed into the receptacle. Cassie was amazed by the contraption, never having seen indoor plumbing before.

"How is this accomplished?"

The maid gave her a friendly smile. "The water is heated in the kitchen downstairs, my lady, before being pumped through a pipe."

"So I may have a hot bath whenever I chose?"

When the maid nodded, Cassie grinned. "I used to have to wait for one of my brothers to haul buckets of water then Mama would spend half the day heating them. She said it was too much work to do more than once a week."

"You may have one every morning if you so wish, my lady."

Cassie shed her robe and nightdress, and then slipped into the steamy warmth of the water with a sigh. If she did not already know better she would say she was in heaven. The lilac scented water soothed away the soreness from her wedding night. The maid encouraged her to recline against the back of the tub and carefully poured water over Cassie's hair.

"What is your name?"

The girl massaged soap into Cassie's long tresses. "My name is Sally, my lady."

"Well, Sally, I suppose I shall have to learn how to host fancy balls and dinner parties."

"His lordship does not have any *soirees* and very few dinner parties."

Cassie waited until Sally rinsed the soap from her hair thoroughly before speaking again. "In truth? He has such a beautiful ballroom. I thought all nobility hosted balls?"

Sally wrung out her hair gently before placing a small cake of lilac scented soap in her hand. "His lordship is too old to indulge in such things."

Cassie soaped her arms thoughtfully. "I know so little about my husband it seems. What does he do with his time?"

Sally shrugged and pulled two towels from the cupboard. "I hear he buys a great many precious artifacts, some from as far away as Egypt."

"Hmm…" Cassie rinsed the soap off and leaned back in the spacious tub. "Is that all he does?"

"I think he spends most of his time in the library reading." Sally held up one of the fluffy white towels.

Cassie stood and stepped from the tub. Sally wrapped a towel around her torso; then wrapped another around her dripping hair. Cassie followed the girl back into her bedroom. Sally helped her dress, and then styled her hair in front of the dressing table mirror with a pair of heated tongs.

"I think I should like to bathe every morning and have you arrange my hair." Cassie watched Sally pin her hair up into artful curls.

Sally smiled. "As you wish, my lady. It is my job to be at your beck and call."

Cassie was astonished. "Truly, anytime I should need you?"

Sally giggled. "Did you never have a maid at home?"

"No, well, we did have a housekeeper of sorts who helped Mama. My father oversees the local parish in our village. I have four sisters and five brothers. I suspect we could not afford a maid." Cassie frowned at her reflection in the mirror. "Why do you suppose his lordship chose to marry me? I mean, I am not a great lady." She sighed. "I am not a lady at all."

Sally smiled. "I am not supposed to gossip, my lady, but he desperately wants an heir."

"The earl has been married three other times, how is it that he has no heir?"

The maid looked around anxiously and whispered, "His first wife died from the sickness within two years of marrying the earl. His second wife lied about being a virgin and soon after the earl found out she ran off with a lover. His third wife was frail, and she never conceived. Five years after they married they say she threw herself down the stairs."

She gasped. "Oh dear, the poor man must have been devastated. Is that why he chose me, the daughter of a simple minister, because I am not frail or sickly?"

Sally shrugged.

"I see." Cassie stood and smoothed her simple blue dress. "I am not sure I like being compared to a broodmare. What about love? Did the earl love any of his other wives, or were they chosen only to bear him children?"

The maid gave her a sad smile. "I heard he did love his first wife, but it is rare, I think, for any noble to marry for love. I believe they usually marry for social position or wealth."

Cassie pondered the situation. It was obvious the earl married her to bear him children, but could she expect him to fall in love with her, or her with him? "Do you suppose the earl might fall in love with me?" she gave voice to her inner thoughts.

"I suppose it is possible." Sally looked at her with an expression of surprise. "How is it you know so little about love?"

"I have never been in love. I suppose I am a little naive, I am the eldest you see. I have been busy helping my father. Mama said she loved Father the first time she met him, but I do not think I feel that way about the earl. I suppose he frightens me a little."

Sally nodded. "I feel the same way sometimes. He is so old and stern."

"Have you ever been in love, Sally?"

"No, my lady, I cannot say as I have yet, although I hope to fall in love one day."

Cassie smiled and closed her hand over Sally's. "I just know you and I will be good friends. You can help me get the earl to fall in love with me, and I will help you fall in love, too. I desire to be loved by the man I am married to." The first step to earn the earl's love would be to learn his likes and dislikes. Her purpose clear, she stood and smiled at Sally. "I think I am ready to go downstairs."

Sally nodded and guided her to the family dining room.

When Cassie entered, the earl was already seated at the far end of the enormous table. She was relieved to discover the wedding guests had left, and they were alone. She gave him a quick curtsy and sat in the chair a footman held for her.

"I trust your room is satisfactory?" The volume of his voice betrayed his deafness.

"Yes, thank you." Her stomach growled as a plate of fresh fruit and glass of milk were placed before her. "I dislike milk, could I have a cup of chocolate please?"

"What is that you say?" the earl bellowed.

"I dislike milk," Cassie pitched her voice louder. "I asked instead for a cup of chocolate."

"Absolutely not, chocolate is forbidden. The physician recommended a suitable diet for you."

Cassie stared at him in dismay. "I beg your pardon?"

"If you are to bear me a healthy son we must take care to watch you eat properly and not exert yourself overly much."

"I do not like milk."

The earl cast a withering look at her and rapped his cane on the table. "You will do as you are told. I will not tolerate insolence in my house!"

Cassie bit her lip. How dare he speak to her such a manner? Stabbing a piece of fruit with her fork, she counted to ten to control her temper as her mother taught her. She would never make the earl fall in love with her if she lost her temper. It simply was not ladylike.

The earl continued. "Your day has been carefully scheduled. You will rise at the tenth hour every morning. Breakfast will be served at promptly eleven, at twelve you will report to the ballroom for your dance lesson. After a light tea you will retire for a nap. Your afternoon will be spent learning to play the harp and painting. The hour before dinner you may spend in a quiet pursuit of your choice, such as embroidering. You will dress and be ready for dinner at promptly seven p.m., after which you will retire. Of course, you will take your fertility potion, and then await my visit."

Cassie dropped her fork to the table with a clatter. Her faux pas was rewarded by a stern glare from the earl. She stared unseeingly at her plate, fearing she was going to positively die of boredom. Why did the earl dislike her so? Did he treat everyone he knew this way? She bit her lip. There was only one course of action; she would be the meek and mild lady the earl expected. Perhaps she could win his approval and hence his love. With a new found sense of determination, she went upstairs to await the dressmaker.

Chapter Two

Cassie turned her face to the spring sunshine, the stone bench beneath her still held the chill of winter. She ticked off on her fingers the months since her marriage. Seven long months and still she had not managed to receive more than a nod of approval from her husband. Nor had she conceived, she thought with a grimace. He had not come to visit her bed in a little over two months; not that she was complaining. Still it would only be a matter of time before he returned to his single-minded task of siring an heir. With the passing of each month the man became increasingly annoyed and short tempered. Cassie closed her eyes and recalled her own distress three weeks earlier when she discovered her monthly flow had begun yet again.

A tapping caught her attention. She opened her eyes and looked up. The earl was seated in his wheelchair at the window, tapping his cane on the glass and motioning for her to come inside.

Why couldn't she spend one nice spring day outside? With a sigh, she stood. Pressing her lips together, she wandered back inside and climbed the stairs reluctantly. She stepped into his room, dreading the barbed accusations she knew would be forthcoming.

The earl scowled at her, his face pale. "What are you doing outside? Are you trying to catch pneumonia, girl?"

Cassie bit her lip and counted quickly to ten in her head before she answered; afraid any sign of defiance would result in being confined to her room, a favorite punishment of her husband's. "No, my lord, it is so nice outside I thought to take in a little fresh air. I was well bundled."

He snorted. "I saw you with your shawl wide open at the neck, girl. Why are you not taking your afternoon nap?"

"I am not tired, my lord." She clenched her hands in the folds of her skirt.

He shook his finger at her. "Do you think just because I have been ill you can change the routine of my house as you see fit?"

Despite careful stewardship of her reply, she had angered him.

"No, my lord, but…."

"I do not want to hear it." He waved his hand impatiently. "The physician has advised me a trip to the healing waters of Bath would be most beneficial to my health. I have decided we shall leave at the end of the month. Perhaps the warmer climate will be more conducive to conceiving a child, unless, of course, you are already breeding?"

Cassie looked at her feet and shook her head, not wanting to meet the gaze she knew would be icy and accusing. The lengthy silence was filled with blame. *How dare he make me feel as if it is my fault I have not conceived? He is the one who has been too sick to visit my bed these past two months.*

"I am hosting a small dinner party tonight. You will be required to attend. I intend to display my recent acquisition, a rare artifact from an Egyptian tomb."

Cassie's mood brightened at the idea of some entertainment. "Will there be dancing, my lord?"

The earl snorted. "Most assuredly not, girl—imagine dancing at my age! You are expected to look pretty, smile, and be at my side at all times. Do you understand?"

"Yes, my lord," Cassie answered, clasping her hands together in an effort to hide her enthusiasm at the thought of mingling with other people.

He waved her away. "Go on now. I expect you to be ready and waiting at seven sharp, not a minute later."

Cassie nodded. It required a concentrated effort to walk from the room. Once free of the earl's presence, her excitement could not be contained. She bolted down the corridor, heedless of the earl's propensity for moderation. A thought made her pause on the threshold to her room. Would the guests be nice or would they simply tolerate her presence? A tiny sigh escaped her. She did not care; at least she would not have to sit through another dreary private dinner with her husband.

When Sally arrived they looked through the gowns in Cassie's wardrobe. Most of the dresses the earl commissioned she had never even worn. They finally decided on a simple, but elegant, soft pink watered silk with a modest neckline studded with shiny pearl flowers.

After she bathed, Sally helped her with the dress. Cassie turned back and forth in front of the mirror, entranced by the way the material shimmered and rustled when she moved.

"Oh, my lady, you are lovely," Sally gushed.

Cassie giggled. "I feel like a princess in this dress."

"Rightfully so, my lady, you look like one."

Cassie forced herself to turn away from the mirror and sit at the dressing table so Sally could work on her hair. She watched in the smaller mirror as the maid arranged her hair on top of her head, and then pinned it so the golden ringlets trailed elegantly down her back. The woman flushed with excitement looking back at her was a stranger. She blinked, but the image reappeared. "Truly you are a miracle worker, Sally. I did not even recognize myself for a moment."

Sally blushed. "Thank you, my lady."

Cassie stood and slipped her feet into the delicate matching slippers as the earl entered the room. He leaned on the silver-tipped cane, put a quizzing glass to his eye, studied her for a moment, and then nodded his approval.

She cast him a shy look; perhaps she could cajole a more pleasant mood out of the stern man. Taking a deep breath she favored him with a bright smile. "You look very nice, my lord."

The earl gave an arrogant sniff and twitched his waistcoat. "You can always tell the character of a man by the cut of his coat."

Cassie nodded to appease his sense of superiority, and he escorted her downstairs to the large entertaining parlor. She gasped in wonder as they walked through the double doors. A life-size, golden cat statue adorned a large stone pedestal in the centre of the room. Cassie studied it curiously. It crouched on gleaming haunches in a regal pose, the emerald eyes glittering as if it were alive. Cassie half expected it to leap from the pedestal at any moment.

"It is said this is the statue of Queen Cleopatra's cat." The earl snatched her hand away as she reached to touch it. "Cats were thought to have spiritual powers in Egypt. They were, in fact, considered gods. I am the only one to have such a priceless artifact in my possession."

A harsh voice came from behind them. "A priceless artifact such as this belongs in a museum, Everton."

The earl turned with a scowl. "If you had your way the statue would still be in Egypt with those heathens, Ashton."

Cassie tore her gaze from the statue and studied the man in the doorway. He was tall, with dark wavy hair, a lock of which hung enchantingly across his forehead. Irritation sparked in his vivid green eyes, which his easy stance did not reflect. He smiled, showing a set of neat white teeth as he leaned against the door frame with confident grace. With casual flicks of his wrists, he drew off his gloves one finger at a time, giving her a smooth look as he did so.

She had the sudden uneasy feeling his smile hid his true feelings in the earl's presence. He stepped away from the door frame and crossed to where they stood with slow deliberate strides. Taking her small hand in his larger tanned one, he gave her a winning smile, and lifted it to his lips. Cassie's skin tingled as he brushed a light kiss on the back, causing her breath to catch in her throat. He was easily the handsomest man she had ever encountered.

He straightened, the roguish twinkle in his eye alerting her to the fact he had not failed to notice her reaction. "Forgive my rudeness, I am Comté Cohen Ashton, and you must be the lovely Lady Everton. I have heard many tales of your beauty, but none do you justice, my lady."

Cassie smiled and pulled her fingers gently from his grip. "Thank you, you flatter me," she murmured, looking to the earl for approval. Her husband paid her no head.

The earl glowered at the much younger man. "If you are here to try to convince me to donate my latest find to your museum, Ashton, save us both the time and leave."

"Not at all, Everton, I am simply here to see your newest treasure." He winked at Cassie. "I can see why you would wish to hide such a priceless piece. It would be a shame if some handsome young rake should steal her away."

Cassie blushed. *The man is an outrageous flirt.*

"Mind your tongue you insolent whelp," the earl snarled.

She hid her amusement behind her fan when the comté gave her a mock look of contrition. Three older gentlemen entered the room and greeted the earl. Cassie ignored them and watched the comté as he walked a full circle around the artifact. He studied the golden cat with an intense stare for a few minutes. When he looked up and caught her watching, he smiled.

Smiling politely, she turned back to the new arrivals, waiting for her husband to present her. This time her fingers did not tingle as they brushed their lips across the back of her hand. The customary greeting over, they disregarded her as they talked to the earl.

The comté was leaning against the fireplace watching her. He smiled again and she smiled back. There was something about the man that drew her interest. Certainly he was sinfully good looking, but there was something more to him, something she could not quite discern.

Four more middle aged gentlemen arrived, and Cassie was momentarily distracted as she was introduced to each one. Before she could return to her contemplation of the comté, the butler announced dinner was ready to be served in the formal dining room. The earl escorted her and seated her at the foot of the table. He then took his place at the head. Once he was situated, the other gentlemen chose their places.

To Cassie's delight, she found the comté seated to her right and an older gentleman, who she hoped she remembered correctly as Lord Kent, seated to her left. He gave her a brief nod and turned his attention to the conversation concerning the artifact.

Cassie sipped her wine to occupy herself as the men engaged in lively discussion. The unaccustomed tartness of the red beverage thrilled her tongue, and she decided she liked the taste.

The comté's smooth voice interrupted her internal speculation. "Lord Everton has excellent taste in wine."

She looked up. He gave her a gracious look and lifted his wine glass to his lips.

"I suppose so. This is but the second time I have tasted wine," Cassie explained with a perplexed smile.

"Indeed?" He paused to take a sip, watching her over the rim of his glass.

Cassie felt herself flush as she sought an explanation that did not mark her as a child. Finally she sighed and uttered the truth, knowing how unsophisticated it sounded. "My lord insists I should drink milk at dinner."

"Milk?" The comté set down his wine glass and quirked his eyebrow. "I should think you are old enough to partake in a glass of wine or two at dinner if you so choose."

"My lord says drinking milk is better since I, umm we, are trying to conceive." She focused her gaze on her napkin in her lap, immediately regretting her admission. "Oh, dear, I suppose I should not have said that. I am unskilled in social graces, I fear."

The comté chuckled. "Think nothing of it, Lady Cassandra, I find your candid manner delightful and refreshing."

She looked up skeptically.

His smile faded, and his lips pressed into a grim line. "You do know Lord Everton has had three other wives and none ever conceived?"

Cassie nodded. What could she say? He was right. She picked up her glass and finished her wine. Before she returned it to the table a footman hurried to refill it and placed a bowl of turtle soup in front of her.

The comté leaned forward as soon as the footman moved down the table. "He is incapable of fathering a child, old war injury you know," he whispered.

"I beg your pardon?" Cassie felt her face burn at the intimate insinuation.

He gave her a weak smile. "If you are hoping for a child you had better look elsewhere, my dear."

Cassie took a hasty swallow of her wine and almost choked. Setting the glass down quickly, she cleared her throat, and turned her attention to the soup. *Good Lord! Could the man be any crasser?*

"I beg your pardon, Lady Cassandra; I did not mean to be rude."

She glanced up, unsure whether he was amusing himself at her expense.

The comté smiled. "Sometimes I tend to see things from a slightly uncivilized point of view. I suppose it is from spending too many days digging in the dirt, in some of the most uncouth countries in the world."

His words piqued her curiosity. "Digging?"

"Yes, Lord Everton and I share an interest in acquiring rare artifacts. Unfortunately, we do not agree on what to do with them once they are unearthed."

Cassie stirred her soup thoughtfully. "You want to put my husband's Egyptian cat in a museum where everyone can see it, but the earl wants to keep it for himself."

"Yes."

"For what it is worth, I think you are right to want to share it with the world." Cassie spared her husband a quick glance, hoping he had not overheard her comment. The earl gave no indication he had, engrossed as he was in the conversation at the other end of the table. When she looked back to the comté, he inclined his head, and gave her an admiring smile.

"Ah, you are clever, as well as beautiful, Lady Cassandra. If you could persuade the earl to donate the piece to a museum, I would be forever in your debt."

She gave him a tepid smile. "I am sorry, but I am afraid I have no influence over his lordship's decisions. He seems to think me incapable of any thoughts of importance." Frowning at the bitter sound of her own words, she looked away, not meaning to betray her feelings.

"That is truly a pity, Lady Cassandra. You are clearly a very intelligent and underappreciated woman. Tell me, how is it you are married to one so advanced in years as the earl?"

Cassie looked at her bowl. "My father gained much for my family by the match. My mother says it is an honor for a simple parson's daughter to marry a titled man."

The comté placed his hand gently over hers. Cassie avoided his eye.

"Pardon my disrespect when I say your father is a fool. Any man, titled or not, would be honored to have you for a wife," his tone was gentle.

Carefully removing her hand from his she reached for her wine glass. *It would be easy to forgive this man anything.* The earl caught her eye as she raised the glass to her lips and gave her a disapproving look as she downed the contents. Lifting her chin stubbornly she signaled the footman to refill her glass. *I am tired of being treated like a child.*

They ate in silence until the second course of roast pheasant, baby potatoes, and asparagus in white sauce was served.

The comté cleared his throat. "I hear you are to take a trip to Bath. Will this be your first time attending the waters there?"

She speared a small bite of pheasant with her fork before glancing at him. "Yes, as a matter of fact, it will. I have never been far from my home village until I married my husband."

"Did you not go on a grand tour for your honeymoon?"

"No. My husband has been ill." She raised her fork and tasted the meat. The flavor was sweet, reminiscent of peach preserves.

"That is too bad, I am sure you would delight in the many sights Europe has to offer." He sliced a piece of pheasant and popped the morsel into his mouth. Her gaze was drawn to his sensual lips as he chewed thoughtfully. "I shall be taking a trip to Bath as well; perhaps I could call on you there?"

She looked down the table at her husband. He frowned at her, and she dropped her gaze to her plate. "I do not think my husband would approve," she said softly.

"I see. Lord Everton is keeping you hidden away like one of his precious artifacts."

Cassie took another sip of her wine. She felt warm and slightly giddy. "Something like that, I suppose." A movement caught her eye, and she looked up.

Lord Kent waved his fork. "Lord Ashton, did I hear you say earlier you are funding another dig in Rome this year?"

"Yes, as a matter of fact. Last year we found an entire set of pottery, completely preserved."

"You do not say? How extraordinary!" Lord Wendell interjected.

"I believe the museum expert dated the pieces to the time of Julius Caesar himself," Ashton boasted.

"That is fascinating." Cassie leaned forward in her chair. "How does one determine the age of a piece of pottery?"

The comté smiled. "It is a very complicated process involving different instruments and, I suppose, a little educated guessing."

The earl interrupted, "The process is too complicated for a female to understand."

Cassie lowered her eyes demurely to hide her anger at her husband's cutting remark. No one seemed to think anything of the comment, and the discussion of Roman artifacts continued. Pressing her lips together she picked up her spoon and toyed with the candied hothouse peaches in cream before her.

"If you would like, I shall be happy to explain the dating of pottery for you after dinner."

She tilted her head and glanced up, giving the comté a doubtful look. "I would not like to impose on you."

He smiled kindly at her. "It would be my pleasure. It is not often I meet a woman who is interested in anything beyond fashion plates and dancing."

"Thank you, I would like that." Cassie smiled. She looked back down at her dessert as the earl stood and cleared his throat.

"Lady Cassandra, excuse us, we will remove ourselves so you may retire for the night."

The men stood as she rose from her chair. The comté took her hand in his and placed a light kiss on the back. "Your presence will be sorely missed, Lady Cassandra. Until we meet again." He executed a graceful bow and released her hand.

Cassie did not miss the scowl the earl directed at the comté. She mumbled a hasty goodnight and retreated from the dining room.

Sally was waiting when she entered her bedchamber. "Did you enjoy yourself, my lady?"

"Oh, Sally, I met a very nice man. I think he is the kindest, most handsome man I have ever met."

Giving her a bemused smile the maid helped her undress.

Cassie sighed as the maid slipped her nightdress over her head. "I think the earl does not like him much though. He seemed angry the comté spoke with me."

"His lordship is very protective. Perhaps he was jealous?"

"Ha! I do not think the earl likes me enough to be jealous," Cassie muttered.

Sally shrugged. "Bernard left your drink on the table beside your bed and made me promise you would finish it."

Cassie picked up the glass and wrinkled her nose. She gave Sally a mischievous grin over her shoulder, and then, in a fit of spiteful will, she poured it into a vase of spring flowers. "You can assure the blasted butler I drank the fertility potion."

Sally giggled. "Yes, my lady. Is there anything else you require before retiring for the evening?"

"No, thank you, Sally." Cassie returned the cup and climbed into bed. "Perhaps if you are not too tired, I could read the next chapter in Maria Edgeworth's *Castle Rackrent*?"

The maid nodded eagerly; then settled herself atop the covers beside her as was their custom when Cassie read out loud to her during the earl's infirmity. "You know, if his lordship were to catch us he would have a fit of apoplexy," she whispered, with a nervous look at the closed door. "'Tis not proper for us to behave like this."

Cassie shrugged and took the book from under her mattress. "He will not visit me tonight."

She opened the book to the page she previously dog-eared and began to read.

Chapter Three

The figure crept along the corridor, his dark clothing blending into the shades of shadows, and then slipped into the parlor. A single lamp burned on the table across from the Egyptian statue. Its bejeweled eyes winked in the flickering light, as if privy to some immensely wicked secret. The cracks-man moved soundlessly across the carpet and stopped before the pedestal, with bated breath, listening for any sign his presence had been discovered. All was eerily quiet in the mansion. Expelling his pent up breath, the man reached up and closed his glove encased hands around the statue. With a practiced touch he eased the archaic feline from its perch, so loving the thrill of the hunt. The quest for this treasure had been exciting, although as easy as petting its loafing namesake. *Perhaps thrice as risky.*

With a cocky smirk, he paused to listen before tucking the ill-gotten treasure into the satchel at his waist. Pride made him stay his retreat for the briefest second and pat the object before slinking back into the inky recesses of the hallway. The man faded into the dark corridor in the hope of making an inconspicuous exit. Without a sound, the study door opened, spilling a shaft of light into the hall across his path. Caught off guard, he darted into the servant's stairwell. Voices breached the silence.

"…retire for the night, Bernard."

"Yes, my lord."

A second of frustration permeated his calm. *Damn!* The earl should be long in bed by now. The stairwell was not a good place to hide in case a servant happened by. They would surely raise the alarm if an intruder was spotted lurking this late in the evening. Thinking quickly, he slunk up the stairs to the second floor. A smile rode his lips. The rope and grapple in his satchel would come in handy, experience telling him it was best to be prepared for any situation. It would make climbing down from one of the windows on the second floor easy.

Topping the landing, the thief peered down the long hallway. A door closed and footsteps approached the bottom of the staircase. He eased back into the murkiness. The first room on his right would suffice as a hiding place for the moment. With a last nervous glance behind him and a twist of the door handle, he slipped inside, closing it softly behind him. It took only seconds for his eyes to adjust to the meager firelight before locking the door. A pink robe lay across the back of one of the chairs nearest the fire. The female occupant of the room must already be in bed, since the fire had burned down to glowing coals. Silently he crossed the room to the window beside the bed, freezing at a rustling sound accompanied by a soft sigh; then turning and peering at the bed. The curtains were drawn to protect the occupant from drafts. He hesitated before easing the curtain back, the light from the fire cast a pale glow on the sleeping figure. She sighed again and rolled in her slumber toward the edge of the bed.

He leaned closer. The firelight enhanced her delicate beauty as her lips parted. A blonde curl caught in the edge of her sleeping mask, slid free to caress her creamy cheek. He ducked inside the curtain, dropping it back in place.

"My lord?" she murmured, still half in dream hibernation. "I have not readied myself for you. You did not tell me you would visit tonight."

His lips clenched together to keep his amusement in check. *The woman believes I am her ancient husband, come to claim his marriage rights.* The thought of the withered old earl being able to perform any matrimonial act amused him.

A slamming door somewhere downstairs distracted him from his reverie. Footsteps hurried down the hallway outside the bedroom. *Has the missing statue already been discovered?* The front door opened and voices carried from outside. *Damn! If I try to escape out the window now they will surely catch me. I have to find somewhere to hide until I can figure out another route of escape.*

"My lord?"

The woman had rolled onto her back, and now lay stiff, with her arms at her side. *Good Lord! Is she waiting for the decrepit earl to make love to her?*

The hounds outside began to bay. *Already they are searching for my trail. I will have to lie low for a few hours until I can make good my escape, but where?* A glimmer of an idea sparked, and then flamed to life. *Here, with her. As long as the woman thinks I am her husband, I will be safe. No one would think to look for me with her. With the drapes pulled, can I fool the lady?*

Setting his bundle on the floor and easing onto the bed, his fingertips touched the side of her cheek. It was warm and silken. Trailing his fingers down to her lips, she quivered but did not move. It would not be right to exact from her a husband's toll. *She is so beautiful.* His desire to touch her was overpowering.

Leaning forward, he kissed her softly, inviting her tongue to come out and play with his. She sighed with wonder, allowing him to trace her lips before delving into her mouth. His passion fogged mind registered her taste; sweet and intoxicating, like wine. As his tongue danced with hers his fingers teased her sensitive peaks. She moaned, relaxing at his touch.

Did the earl ever touch her like this? It was doubtful. Removing his lips from hers, he rained a little trail of feather-light kisses down the column of her throat to her other breast. She gasped when his lips closed over the peak through the thin material of her nightdress, making him sure she never experienced anything like it in the months she had been married. When his stimulation stopped she whimpered in protest. Placing a hand on either side of her thighs he began to ease her nightdress up. She shivered as the silky material slipped across her breasts and over her head. Before she could protest, the garment was off. It fluttered to the floor in a whisper of satin. *The earl probably never wanted her naked before, the old man seemed far too frigid for that.*

"My lord?"

Her breathless enquiry made him smile. "Shh."

In order to silence any further protests, a kiss sealed her lips. She reached for him, he caught her hands, pinning them gently above her head, releasing them when she relaxed. They stayed above her head when his fingers slid down her arm, along the side of her breast where his other hand returned to playing, and then down across her hip to the indent of her naval. She inhaled as the pad of his thumb traced a lazy circle there for a moment. Switching his mouth to her other breast, his tongue traced a similar pattern to which had already been bestowed on its twin. She gasped, stiffening, letting his fingers slide leisurely into her soft Aphrodite's mound.

"My lord, you must not. 'Tis not proper."

Her breathy voice made him smile. "Shh." The word whispered against her breast, making her shiver. She moaned as his breath brushed over her sensitive nipples.

Wiggling slightly, she moaned again as his fingers slid further down until they touched her sensitive bud nestled in the downy hair. With a sharp inhale she clenched her legs together on his hand. He returned his attention to her breast until she surrendered; then slid his fingers between her slick, damp folds. She whimpered, clutching his arm. Moving his lips back to cover hers and silence her arousal, he vowed not to take her. It was enough to show her what her body was capable of, but, oh, how he wanted her. His hands shook with his desire to have her for himself.

She quivered as his fingers caressed her sensitive bud, allowing her hands to slip down and grip his shoulders. The frown puckering her cupid's lips betrayed her confusion. She knew the touch was not the earl's, he suspected, so what would she do now? Without waiting for her reaction to this new discovery, he rolled her sensitive bud between his fingers. She cried out against his lips, arching toward his hand. Panting, she rocked her hips in rhythm with his stroking fingers.

The tension built in her sweet body, and when he was certain she could not bear the feeling any longer, he shifted his weight. Despite his vow to refrain from bedding her, his resolve broke. Her response to him fueled his desire beyond control. Freeing his member from his breeches, he slid it into her in one quick thrust. Tearing her lips from his, she cried out. Settling into a steady rhythm, a thousand fireworks exploded in his head. Bucking her hips to fulfil her release, she moved in unison with him. The lady stiffened beneath him. A low, animal-like growl erupted from his throat, releasing his pent up passion as she sagged against the mattress, her breathing as ragged as his own.

He withdrew and rolled to the side, drawing her to his chest, and cradling her there. The flowery sent of her perfume mingled with his own spicy cologne and tickled his nose. *I did not mean to take her. It was so wrong, but it felt so right.* She lay in his embrace for a moment, and then flailed, struggling to get up. He held her fast.

Her voice rose, choked with terror. "Let go of me!"

"Hush or they will hear."

She continued her struggles, and he winced when she caught him in the side with her knee.

"Who are you? How *dare* you touch me?"

Sliding his leg across hers he clamped a hand over her mouth, "Shh. You will wake the whole house, and I have no wish to spend the rest of my life in Newgate."

She whimpered, but stopped her struggles.

"I will take my hand from your mouth if you promise not to scream." When she nodded he slowly lifted his hand.

An angry hiss of air followed her sharp intake of breath. "Who are you, and what do you want with me?"

"I am a friend. It was not my intention to frighten you."

"A friend would not force himself on a lady."

He chuckled at the bitter edge to her voice. "I did not have to force you, my lady. Your sweet body begged me to make love to you."

"Is making love what you call accosting a sleeping woman in her own bed?"

"Have you never been made love to by a man before?"

"I-that is, well, I am married."

A knowing grin touched his lips. "That does not answer my question. Does your husband kiss you and make you cry out for his touch?"

"No," she admitted, reluctance tainting her voice.

"Then I am the first to make love to you."

"Why?" Her question was voiced so quietly it was almost inaudible.

He stroked her cheek gently. "I could not help myself. You are so beautiful and innocent. I could not bear to think of you lying beneath that withered old man as he rutted. You deserve to feel the pleasure a real man can give you."

"I have betrayed my husband," she cried, her voice brimming

with horror.

"No. You have not betrayed him, your body betrayed you. The earl will never know, and you shall have a memory to cherish each time you must endure his attentions." His intention had been to console her, but she stiffened as his lips found hers again in the dark. He captured her hands in his when she pushed against his chest, nipping seductively at her lower lip. She softened, his tongue slid into her mouth to tease. She gasped, her body trembling slightly. With reluctance he broke off the kiss and released her hands.

Her fingers came to rest passively against his chest. "How do you do that?"

"Do what?" His lips twitched at the wonder in her breathless enquiry. His hand slid down to stroke her breast, and she responded by arching her back and pressing her soft flesh against his hand. His lips moved to pleasure her other breast, and she seized the bed clothes in her hands giving in to his ministrations.

The mattress dipped as he sat up, swung his legs over the side, and buttoned his trousers. "I regret I must leave you now, my lady."

When she opened her mouth to protest, he kissed her lips gently before ducking through the bed curtains; turning around as she sat up and slipped off her mask. The glow of the fire lent a rosy flush to her skin. Her hair hung loose around her like a glowing shroud. Eyes glazed with passion, she clutched the bed clothes around her chin. He reached behind and opened the window without taking his gaze from her enchanting form. A breeze stole through the room, causing the bed curtains to flutter wildly. Pivoting, he clamped his grappling hook over the windowsill and tossed down the rope. Straddling the ledge he scooped up the satchel, and then blew her a kiss before lowering himself to the ground. With a flick of his wrist, the grapple fell from its place. He slung it over his shoulder and jogged toward the hedge-lined drive with distracting memories of the evening's chance encounter swirling in his thoughts.

Chapter Four

Cassie slid from the bed, snatched up her nightdress, and padded barefoot to the window. Slipping the garment over her head, she peered into the darkness. There was no sign of the mysterious stranger. Was she dreaming? Pinching herself, she flinched; then frowned. No, she was definitely awake. She almost wished it was a dream, for dreams returned and had no consequences or guilt.

She jumped when someone pounded on her door.

"Cassandra!" the earl bellowed from the other side.

"Yes, my lord?" she answered, before hastily shutting the window. *If the earl demands entrance to my room would he know or suspect what happened?*

"Did you hear anything within the house?"

"No, my lord."

"Be sure to keep your door locked."

"Yes, my lord." Cassie waited until she heard his footsteps recede down the passageway before returning her gaze to the window. Pressing her face to the glass, she squinted into the dark, seeing nothing but shadows. Confused, she turned away and climbed back into bed. The subtle scent of the stranger's cologne still lingered as she replayed the encounter over and over in her mind, struggling to convince herself she had not enjoyed the man's caress.

I am sinful! What would my father say? I am supposed to be a pious and faithful daughter. I have shamed myself and my family. Why did the mysterious stranger sneak into my room? Did he sense my sinful longing and seek to take advantage of it?

The sun was painting the sky various shades of pink when sleep finally claimed her.

* * * *

"My lady?"

Cassie snuggled further into the bed clothes.

"My lady?"

She groaned, not wanting to emerge from her dreamy cocoon. "What is it?"

"You have overslept," Sally said from the bedside.

Cassie sat up, her body feeling achy and limp. She could have sworn she just fell asleep. Blinking, she looked out the window. The sun was already shining with promise in the mid morning sky.

"Are you feeling alright, my lady?"

She yawned. "I am a bit tired." *And guilt-ridden, embarrassed....*

"Shall I have your breakfast sent up and tell his lordship you are indisposed this morning?"

Cassie smiled. "Umm, that would be lovely, Sally, thank you."

After the maid left, Cassie swung her legs over the side of the bed and slipped on her wrapper. A tell-tale heat crept up her neck and flushed her cheeks when she recalled the events from the night before. Was she really visited in the night by a stranger who made love to her? The tingle between her legs made the question horribly redundant. Would her husband be able to tell she had lain with another man? She felt a twinge of guilt. *The earl must never find out! He would surely cast me out, or worse....*

The familiar thump of the earl's cane in the hall alerted Cassie to his approach, and she hurried back to bed, scrambling under the covers before the door opened.

He crossed the room and fixed her with a stern stare. "Your maid tells me you are ill this morning."

She lowered her gaze to the bed covers and plucked at a loose thread on the satin spread.

"Too much excitement last night," the earl concluded. "I think I will cancel the trip to Bath. I would not want it to overexert you."

"Oh, no. Please, my lord. I am only a little tired this morning, nothing to be worried about," she hurried to reassure him, unwilling to forgo the much anticipated trip.

The earl contemplated her for a moment, his thin white brows bunching. "Very well, you will rest in bed today. Your maid can pack for you, and if you are refreshed by then, we shall leave the day after tomorrow."

Cassie nodded. He gave her another careful look, and then left the room. She leaned back against the pillows, her stomach churning as she swallowed her guilt.

Sally entered a few minutes later with a breakfast tray which she set carefully across Cassie's lap. Upon lifting the silver lid she grinned. "Bernard was not around this morning so I took the opportunity to slip you a cup of chocolate."

"Oh, Sally you are such a treasure." Cassie picked up the steaming cup and sipped the hot chocolate slowly, savoring the rich flavor. *Today was a special day in deed.* A whole day to herself with no silly schedule to adhere to and a cup of her favorite treat. She sobered when she recalled the reason for her reprieve.

"A trip is just the thing you need, my lady." The maid chattered on, sorting through the wardrobe and packing it.

Cassie ignored her cheerful prattle as she sought to put a face to the stranger. Try as she might, she could conjure nothing beyond a shadowy form and a husky voice. An inkling of something familiar pricked her recollections. *Do I know the man? He seemed to know me or at least of me.*

"...the commotion around here last night must have kept you up."

Cassie blinked and focused her gaze on the maid carefully folding a petticoat. *What was it she was saying about a commotion?* "What commotion?"

Sally placed the garment in the bottom of a large trunk; then glanced at her and reached for some tissue. "A thief stole the earl's Egyptian artifact late last night."

"Really?" Cassie's heart skipped a beat as she recalled the stranger telling her to be quiet or he might end up in Newgate. He had not been afraid of being caught in bed with her; he had been afraid of being caught stealing the earl's artifact. The scoundrel could have at least had the decency to be repentant for his misdeed where she was concerned. Her face heated. "Did they catch the man responsible for the theft?"

The girl shook her head and placed paper between the folds of a delicate muslin dress. "No. No one seems to know who it was."

Cassie's thoughts flickered with the flames of the fire. Had she screamed, the household would have been alerted to the thief's presence in her bedchamber. The earl lost his priceless treasure because of her. If he found out he would be furious. Cassie nibbled on a piece of toast from the tray. If the thief was caught, would he tell of her deception and infidelity? Her hands shook, and she tried to ignore the fear gripping her in icy fingers.

"Do you think it might have been one of the earl's guests who stole the artifact?" Cassie wondered out loud.

Sally glanced at her. "It could have been, but the earl seemed to think it was the work of a professional thief. No one saw him enter or leave the house."

Cassie felt sick to her stomach. Not only did she betray her husband, she did so with a professional thief. The man was probably very dangerous, and she had given herself to him like a common trollop. She closed her eyes and prayed God would forgive her for her terrible sins. Perhaps God would punish her by denying her a babe. She might have to endure the earl's disgusting attentions for years. Was it wrong to wish the earl's touch had the same effect on her as the mysterious stranger's? With a groan she pushed the breakfast tray off her lap and shrank under the covers.

Confusion addled her mind. It was wrong of her to lay with a man who was not her husband, but it felt so good...Why did her husband's touch repulse her when a complete stranger's turned her inside out? She should be mortified by her behavior, but all she could think of was his lips brushing hers, how her body tingled at his slightest touch. Was she completely immoral?

"My lady?"

She poked her head out from under the covers. "Yes, Sally?"

The maid's brows furrowed with concern. "Are you feeling alright?"

Cassie moaned and hid her face behind her hands. "Oh, Sally. I have done something terrible." The mattress sagged as Sally perched on the edge of the bed.

"Whatever it is you have done, it cannot be so bad."

"It is horrible, Sally. I am a truly terrible person."

"You have a kind heart, my lady. I do not believe you could do anything bad."

Cassie sobbed even harder. "Oh, Sally, I *have* done something unforgivable."

Sally took her hand and patted it gently. "We are friends, are we not?" When Cassie looked up and nodded through her tears the maid continued, "Then you can trust me to help you. Tell me what it is you have done you think is so terrible. I promise I will keep it a secret until I die." She made an "X" across her heart with her fingers.

Cassie wiped the tears from her face with her sleeve. "My husband will never forgive me for what I have done."

"Then we shall never tell him," Sally vowed.

Cassie sniffed. "I drank too much wine at dinner even though I knew it would anger the earl. I was abed when I was awakened by a man in my room. At first I thought it was my husband, but then he touched me and made me feel things I never felt before. When I realized it was not my husband I should have screamed, but I did not because I did not want him to stop." She began to cry again. "Do you not see Sally? I allowed the thief to steal more than my husband's artifact, and I helped him escape. Lord Everton will surely cast me out or have me arrested. I betrayed him. I betrayed God and my father, too!"

Sally hugged her gently. "No, his lordship will not cast you out, my lady, because we will not tell him."

"What if the man is arrested and he tells my husband what I did?"

The corners of Sally's brown eyes crinkled as she worried her lower lip between her teeth for a moment, and then she smiled. "I shall tell him the man is a liar. I was with you all night and did not see anyone come into your chamber."

"You would do that for me?" Cassie wiped her tears on the corner of the bedspread.

"Of course, I would." Sally smiled. "Now get some rest and do not fret. Soon we will be in Bath. I am so excited! I have never been outside of London."

Chapter Five

Cassie followed the earl up the gangplank of the monstrous ship. "Oh, look! What are those big grey animals over there? Have you ever seen such strange creatures?" She leaned over the railing and pointed with her fan.

The earl rapped the rail with his cane. "Control yourself, girl! Hang onto the railing lest you fall overboard."

Biting back her rebuttal she gripped the railing, glancing fleetingly at the choppy water below.

"Those are elephants." A masculine voice from behind startled her. "They are part of Astley's new show." Cassie pivoted, keeping a hand on the rail. The comté was making his way up the gangplank.

He smiled. "Have you never seen one before?"

She smiled back; then cast her eyes downward for fear the earl would find fault with her for welcoming the comté in such a way. "No."

"It is a pleasure to see you again, Lady Everton." He took her hand, bowed, and placed a light kiss on the back of it.

Cassie was almost sorry her gloves were the recipient of his caress. He straightened with a delighted look, the skin around his eyes crinkling with good humor. It seemed the man was always smiling, as if he found the world and its inhabitants constantly amusing.

Tucking her hand in the crook of his arm, he took her parasol, and held it protectively above her. He escorted her up the ramp to the main deck, nodding to the earl who stood waiting with a displeased look on his face. "Everton," he acknowledged with a tip of his head.

"Ashton." The earl frowned stiffly at Cassie before turning to his nemesis. "What are you doing here?"

He released Cassie's hand, but continued to shade her with the parasol. "I am going to Bath to take in the waters, the same, I presume, as you."

The earl merely grunted, taking Cassie's hand. "Come along girl, we best settle in our stateroom before the ship sets sail." Rudely snubbing the comté he practically dragged her away.

When she peeked over her shoulder, Ashton tipped his hat and grinned. The sun's rays highlighted his dark hair with light bluish streaks she never noticed before. His tanned skin left no doubt he was of robust health. The comté was a picture of manly perfection. She glanced at the earl out of the corner of her eye. *Unlike my frail husband.*

Sally was waiting in their stateroom. The sitting room was large and elegantly furnished. It contained a settee, two comfortable looking armchairs, a bookshelf full of leather bound volumes, and a small card table on which sat a box of chess pieces. A door on the left wall opened to reveal the earl's bedroom. Cassie grimaced at the thought and followed Sally through a similar door on the right, leading to her own room.

The bed hung on thick chains swaying gently with the subtle rocking of the ship. The only other items in the room were a wardrobe in the corner, beside which an oriental dressing screen and a washstand were placed.

Enchanted, Cassie wandered over to one of the two small round windows and peered out the portholes to the wharf below. Well dressed gentlemen mixed with the sailors and dock workers hurrying about their business. Reluctantly, she turned away from the scene as the earl addressed her.

"Dinner is at seven. I will come to collect you then."

As he twisted with his awkward gait to leave, Cassie placed her hand on his arm to stop him. "May I stand on deck and watch when we leave port?"

He scowled at her fingers resting on his finery. "It is much too dangerous for a girl to be wandering the deck alone. You will stay in your rooms unless you are with me. Is that clear?"

Cassie nodded and removed her hand. It was disappointing she would have as little freedom here as at home.

The earl left, the key scraping in the lock. She wandered back to the window as the ship shuddered and a whistle blew. *How dangerous could it be to watch as they sailed from port on the deck if the earl is with me?*

She clutched the window frame, bracing her feet as the ship began to move along the channels down the River Thames. The little porthole from which she viewed their departure restricted her enjoyment of the sights. She turned away in disappointment and meandered back to the sitting room, trailing her fingers along the smooth walls of the stateroom. Sally was seated in one of the chairs, carefully mending a stocking. With a small pout she crossed the room and flopped into the chair opposite the maid.

"I thought being on a ship would be an exciting adventure, but there is nothing to do. The earl insisted he could not possibly endure a bouncing coach trip to Bath, but I fear it would have been more enjoyable than this."

Sally looked up from her mending. "There are many books on the shelf. Perhaps one of them would interest you?"

Cassie shook her head. "Reading always makes me sleepy." She slouched, resting her elbow on the arm of the chair with her chin cupped in her hand.

The maid smiled. "If you like I could teach you how to sew to pass the time."

"Would you?" Cassie asked, her mood brightening at the idea of having something worthwhile to do.

Sally shrugged. "Sure. Here, 'tis easy." She passed the needle and thick thread to Cassie. "Let me show you a few of the simpler stitches."

The afternoon flew by as Cassie concentrated on learning the new skill. Before she knew it, it was time to dress for dinner. She chose a deep blue velvet evening gown, and Sally pinned her hair up in her favorite cascade of curls. Satisfied her appearance was in order, she paced back and forth waiting for the earl. Finally the door to his bedchamber opened, and he hobbled in, dressed in formal dinner attire.

He gave her a once over and nodded his approval. "Well, then, let's go girl. Mind you keep to one glass of wine tonight so you do not embarrass yourself like the last dinner party."

Cassie bit her lip to hold back her retort. It would do no good to tell him she had not embarrassed herself; it would only make him surly. He might think to forbid her to leave her room for the remainder of the voyage. The earl exited the sitting room, and she followed meekly.

The dining room was as large as the earl's she discovered. The massive oak table stretched from one end of the room to the other and was bolted to the floor.

The captain, a rather short, older man, rose from his seat at the head of the table and raised her hand to his lips. His salt and pepper beard tickled her fingers. "I am Captain Maxim Winters, and you must be the lovely Lady Everton." He dropped her hand and gestured to a seat on his left. "I would be honored if you would sit beside me."

She nodded and took her seat. The earl sat opposite her on the captain's other side, passing her a warning scowl as the other guests began to file in. To her disappointment they all seemed to be nearly as old as the earl, except for Comté Ashton who took an empty seat a few chairs down and across the table.

The captain was friendly and attentive as course after course was brought out and consumed. Cassie was careful to keep her responses polite and sedate. She glanced up at the earl a number of times during the meal and did not detect any annoyance towards her behavior. If she played the part of a demur lady perhaps the earl would be pleased enough to allow her some freedom on the ship.

An elderly lady seated across from Cassie addressed her, "Is this your first trip to Bath, my dear?"

"Yes, it is." Cassie smiled politely. "The physician thought it might be good for my husband to take in the healing waters."

The woman nodded. "How right he is. There is nothing better for what ails one."

"I thought it might settle my young wife," the earl interjected. "You know it is difficult for one so young and flighty to settle into her wifely duties."

Cassie's cheeks burned at the earl's cutting remark. She looked down at her plate as the other gentlemen snickered. *Must the fault for all things lie with me?*

"The young ladies these days are a little like young thoroughbreds," another gentleman explained. "One must rein them in until they have a few miles on them, then they settle down to an acceptable pace."

"Here, here," said another. "I do not know how you do it, Everton, keeping a lovely young filly like yours happy and content."

The earl affected a superior look. "A strict schedule does the trick. Keeping them busy and their minds on bearing babes is the secret."

A chorus of chuckles pricked her anger. *Self-righteous cads!*

As if sensing her discomfort the comté came to her rescue. "It has been my experience one as gentle and sweet natured as Lady Everton hardly needs reining in."

Cassie gave him a small grateful smile.

The comté dipped his head slightly in acknowledgement. "I had the pleasure of dining at Lord Everton's home. He is a lucky man, indeed, to have such a lovely young wife."

"Speaking of wives, Lord Ashton, are you ever going to quit playing in the dirt and find yourself some lovely young thing to spend the rest of your days with?" the elderly lady across from Cassie peered at him through her looking glass.

Cassie barely hid her grin as the man blushed and pretended interest in a piece of potato on his plate. "Alas, Lady Wendell, I have yet to find an unwed lady who can hold a candle to the excitement of finding a rare artifact. Rest assured if there comes a day when such a fascinating lady captures my attention, she will definitely be worth pursuing."

Everyone at the table tittered.

The earl stood with a sour look. "Lady Everton, if you please, it is time for us gentlemen to have our port and cigars. I will escort you back to your room."

Cassie stood. "Goodnight, everyone." She favored the comté with a bright smile, prepared to bear her husband's scathing tongue for it, and followed the earl back to her room.

To her surprise, the earl refrained from chastising her as he opened the door to their stateroom. "I shall be late tonight so do not wait up. You may expect me to resume my nightly visits to your bed tomorrow evening at the usual time." He ushered her inside the sitting room without waiting for her to answer and left, locking the door behind him.

Chapter Six

Cassie awoke the next morning feeling as if her stomach was hosting a revolt. She moaned, rolled over, and curled into a fetal position. Closing her eyes, she tried to ignore the offending rocking motion of the ship.

"Sally?"

Upon receiving no answer she opened her eyes. The small cot the maid slept on was neatly made up. Cassie clapped her hand over her mouth as her stomach rolled. She bolted from the bed to the chamber pot where she promptly unloaded the contents of her stomach. She huddled on the floor until she was reasonably sure the worst was over before crawling to the open door of the sitting room. The maid was not there either. Miserable and weak, she rested her head on the door frame, gathering the strength to return to her bed.

A knock sounded on the stateroom door. Staggering to her feet, she made her way across to see who was there. When she turned the knob she was surprised to find it unlocked. She swung the door open.

"Sally, where have you been? I feel terrible…." she trailed off, staring at Comté Ashton who stood in the open doorway.

"I am sorry if I am intruding, Lady Everton." He paused when she leaned against the door to steady herself. "You really are sick. Why are you not in bed?"

Cassie glared at him. "There was no one else to answer the door."

He glanced over his shoulder before stepping past her into the room. After shutting the door he led her to the settee. Once she was seated, he marched to her room, disappearing inside. A moment later he came back with a thick wool blanket which he spread across her lap and tucked in around her.

"You do not have to take care of me, my lord." She submitted to his administrations, too weak to offer any resistance.

"I am here, and I do not see anyone else to care for you." He poured some water into a basin, dunked his handkerchief and wrung it out. Kneeling on the floor beside her feet, he folded the wet cloth and tenderly laid it across her forehead.

Cassie moaned. "I feel wretched."

"You look it." When she glowered at him he grinned. "Do not worry, my dear, you are not the first person to get seasick you know."

"Is that what is wrong with me? Are you sure it is not something more serious? Perhaps I am dying."

The comté chuckled. "Never fear, although many a great man has fallen prey to seasickness, none I know ever perished from it."

Despite her wretched condition, Cassie giggled.

The outer door opened and Sally entered carrying a breakfast tray. She paused on the threshold when she saw the two of them. "My lady?"

"Sally, I have been looking for you."

The maid hurried into the room and placed the tray on the card table. "Is everything alright, my lady?"

Ashton nodded. "Your mistress is just a little seasick."

Cassie groaned. "A little?"

His upper lip twitched, his eyes twinkling with amusement. "I stand corrected; your mistress is very seasick." He gave Cassie a small bow. "I see sufficient help has arrived so I will beg your leave."

"Wait." Cassie held the cloth to her head as she sat up to keep it in place. "You came to see me for something?"

"Actually I came to see your husband."

"Oh," she mumbled, disappointed he had not come to see her, but at the same time feeling guilty she wanted him to say such a thing.

"What about, or do you make a habit of consorting with half-naked married women in their parlors?" the earl asked. Scowling furiously, he limped into the room.

Cassie's face heated when she realized she answered the door clad in only a thin nightdress.

"Your wife answered the door as her maid was occupied. I merely helped her to the settee since she is so obviously seasick." The comté cast her a sympathetic look.

The earl glared at her. "Where was your maid?"

She looked down at her hands and wrung the edge of the blanket.

"She was getting me a breakfast tray, my lord. I thought it was her when I answered the door." Of all the moments for her husband to show up; she couldn't look any guiltier in his eyes unless she had her arms around the man's neck.

The comté cleared his throat. "I came to speak to you about a piece of pottery my team discovered this year. I understand you have in your collection a similar one, entirely intact. Perhaps we can discuss it somewhere else so we will not disturb your wife."

The earl walked with Ashton to the door. "I do not see what there is to discuss, but if you must, we can talk in the card room."

He gave Cassie a polite bow. "I hope you are feeling better soon, Lady Everton." The man turned smartly and preceded the earl out the door.

Cassie sighed when the door shut behind the two men. "Oh, Sally, I have done it again. Every time I behave in a way the earl approves of, I do something irresponsible and make him angry with me."

"It is my fault, my lady," Sally wailed. "I should not have left you alone. I did not know you were sick. I will tell his lordship it was my wrongdoing."

"You did nothing incorrect. If you tell Lord Everton it is your fault he might fire you then I would be all alone. You are my only friend. If I take the blame what is the worst my husband can do, other than lock me in my room for the rest of the trip?"

Sally looked doubtful as she took the lid off the tray. The smell of bacon and eggs wafted to Cassie and her stomach threatened to rebel again. Clamping a hand over her mouth, she leaped off the settee, making a mad dash for the chamber pot. After retching she climbed back into bed and curled up in a ball of misery.

"I will take your breakfast back to the galley and see about getting you some toast and weak tea," she heard the maid say from the bedchamber door.

"Good idea," Cassie mumbled.

* * * *

By later in the evening Cassie's stomach settled somewhat. She still felt queasy and weak but well enough to nibble on some bland biscuits and drink some weak tea. She was propped up in bed reading a book on Rome when the earl entered her bedchamber.

He crossed to her bedside. "I see you are still feeling under the weather."

Cassie set the book in her lap. "Yes, my lord."

His eyes narrowed, and he scrutinized her carefully as if searching for some indication of falsehood on her part. "Odd, I did not think you would be the type to get seasick. One might expect it from a true blue-blooded lass, but not one of such a sturdy stock as yourself."

"I am sorry to disappoint you, my lord," Cassie muttered.

"Well, I suppose it cannot be helped. Perhaps it is for the best you stay confined to your room for the remainder of the voyage."

The prospect of staying in her room, no matter how ill, was daunting. "Mayhap some fresh sea air might just do the trick, my lord."

"I doubt that. As for your marriage bed duties, I will have to give you a reprieve until you are feeling better."

"Thank you," Cassie mumbled, careful to keep her relief from showing.

"You will take care to stay away from that scoundrel, Ashton. You are not to admit him to your rooms under any circumstances, do I make myself clear?"

"Yes, my lord, but nothing happened. He was just trying to be kind—"

"You were alone, half-clothed, in a room with a notorious rake," the earl bellowed.

Cassie cringed. He made it sound worse than it was. He was angry with her, again.

"I will send that maid of yours packing as soon as we dock."

She felt her face drain of blood. "Please do not send Sally away, it was not her fault. I should not have opened the door." *Sally is the only friend and comfort I have. I cannot allow the earl to send her away. Allow? As if I have the power to allow anything....*

The earl leaned forward on his cane as if to emphasize his words. "If you ever talk to Ashton again, I shall dismiss the girl immediately."

Relief swamped her. "Yes, my lord."

He turned and left the room. Cassie waited until she heard the sitting room door slam shut before retrieving the book from her lap. She read with every intention of concentrating on the words, however her wayward thoughts wandered back to the comté. *The man is handsome and kind. He treats me with respect. I wish the earl was more like him. Why does my husband dislike me so much? He treats me like a small, naughty child. Perhaps the earl's attitude towards me will change once I bear him a child....*

Sally entered the bedchamber, her expression somber. "Thank you, my lady."

"You are welcome, Sally." Cassie closed her book and set it on the bedside table. "I am so stiff from lying about all day. I wish I could go for a walk."

"His lordship will be engaged in a card game on the upper deck for a few hours yet. We could sneak out for a stroll and he would be none the wiser," she said with a mischievous gleam in her eye while pulling Cassie's blue cloak out of the wardrobe.

"I do not know, Sally, my husband will be furious if he finds out I disobeyed him. He is already angry with me." She sighed wistfully and looked longingly at the door. *A walk would be lovely.*

The maid handed her the cloak. "We will stay on the main deck and take a quick walk around. We will be back in your room in ten minutes, I promise."

Cassie slid from the bed. "All right." With a conspiratorial grin she allowed the maid to help her dress in a warm wool day dress, matching slippers, and cloak.

When she was ready, Sally opened the sitting room door, peering cautiously into the passage way before she beckoned to Cassie. Together they slipped out the door and hurried down the deserted corridor, past the stairs to the upper level, and onto the open deck.

Cassie took a deep breath of cool sea air and tilted her head back to look up at the heavens. The sky was pin-cushioned with what seemed like millions of miniscule glittering lights. "Have you ever seen so many stars, Sally?"

"No." Sally's breathless whisper mirrored Cassie's own awe.

They linked arms as they strolled along the softly rolling deck.

The moon lit a wide white smear across the sea. They stopped by the ship's rail to watch the waves as they glistened and undulated gently in the moonlight.

"I see you are feeling better."

Cassie spun around to find the comté standing behind them. "You startled me!"

"Then I am sorry, it was not my intention," he said softly. Taking her hand in his, he lifted it, turned it over, and placed a kiss on her palm.

Cassie shivered, her fingers tingling at his touch. When he straightened she pulled her hand from his and turned away to put a little distance between him and her pounding heart. "I have to go."

The comté stepped in front of her, blocking her path. "Have I done something to offend you?"

Cassie darted a glance around the deck, afraid someone might see and tell the earl. "No. I have to go. I should not be here with you."

"You are perfectly safe with me. With your maid in attendance there is no shame in talking," he consoled her.

"I am not entirely sure of that," Cassie mumbled.

Ashton laughed. "Ah, I see you have heard of my reputation as an incorrigible rake. I assure you it is all embellishments on behalf of a few spurned ladies and their jealous suitors."

"I must go," Cassie insisted. "My husband will be angry with me for being out here talking with you. He has forbade it."

"I see." His face sobered as he contemplated her. "At least allow me to escort you the rest of the way around the ship. The earl is engaged in a lively card game at the moment so I am sure he will not notice your absence for a while longer."

"No, really, I must go. I do not want to incur my husband's wrath."

He frowned at her briefly, the concern in his eyes easy for her to read. "Will Lord Everton beat you for disobeying?"

"No." Cassie could not help wondering if perhaps a beating would be better than being locked away for disobedience. She shuddered.

He gave her a winning smile. "Then what harm is there in a quick stroll?"

Relenting, she took his offered arm. Sally hurried ahead at a respectful distance as they strolled along in silence. Cassie inhaled deeply, trying to ignore the warmth of the comté's arm under her hand, his spicy sent filling her nostrils. *Where have I smelled that fragrance before? Perhaps the Earl's dinner party...* Her heart thumped so hard against her ribs she was certain he could hear it over the soft swish of the waves.

He glanced down at her as if he could hear her thoughts. "Are you still feeling seasick?"

She nodded. "Terribly so, I am afraid."

"I will ask the captain to send you some ginger root tea in the morning. It will help."

"Why are you so nice to me?" Cassie wondered out loud.

He regarded her solemnly for a moment before he answered. "You deserve to be treated nicely. You seem so sad and lonely."

"And you feel obligated to rescue bits of broken pottery and lonely ladies?" she asked, allowing a trace of ridicule to color her tone.

He chuckled. "Some things need to be unearthed, polished, and treasured."

What would it be like to be treasured by the comté? Would he make love to me as the stranger had? Would he cater to my every whim and profess his love with trinkets and lovely words?

He favored her with a knowing grin. "I suspect you are wondering what it would be like to be treasured and treated like the desirable woman you are."

Cassie swallowed. *How can he sense my thoughts?* "I am sure my husband treasures me in his own way," she said, in a noble attempt to convince herself.

The comté stopped and drew her to him. "Does he treasure your thoughts or just your womb?"

Cassie gasped. "I am more than just a-a vessel to bear my husband's heir," she protested without conviction.

"You do not believe that any more than I, Cassandra," he whispered.

She shivered as he ran his hands along the small of her back, pulling her to him. Her breath caught in her throat as she looked up at his face, shrouded in shadow. Then his lips were on hers. Cassie sighed, leaning toward him. *I should not let him kiss me.*

With a low groan he wrapped his hand in her hair, crushing her to him, his kiss tender but demanding. His embrace was somehow familiar and safe, but strange and dangerous at the same time. Cassie shuddered as her body grew uncomfortably warm.

He pulled back and whispered, "I had to see you again. I cannot forget you."

Jerking from her trance she pushed frantically against his chest. "Let me go this instant!"

He released her with a groan. "I am sorry. I did not mean to—"

"Oh, my, God! I am disgraceful. The earl is right to keep me locked away in my room." With a wail of dismay Cassie fled back to her room.

Chapter Seven

The next morning Cassie huddled in bed trying to ignore the waves of nausea engulfing her. She deserved to be seasick. God was punishing her for being a loose and wanton woman. When she scrambled from the bed to hang over the chamber pot she promised she would be a better wife to the earl, if God would only ease her suffering. An hour later when she stumbled back to her bed, she swore there was no God.

She heard Sally's tread on the carpet. "My lady?"

"Go away." Cassie moaned, burying her head under the covers.

"I have the tea the comté promised you."

"I do not want to hear about him, it is his fault I am sick. I am being punished by God for wanting him." *Yes, it is all his fault...well not really.* Just this once might she blame him?

"I do not think your seasickness is a punishment from God," Sally admonished.

"How do you know?" Cassie sniffled. "My father is a minister and he told me God punishes those who sin."

"I do not think a kiss is that big a sin, surely God has other more important sins to demand repentance for," Sally pointed out with a trace of humor in her voice.

"Are you making fun of me?" Cassie demanded crossly.

"No. Why not sit up and try the cup of tea? The comté thought it might help. What can it hurt to try it?"

"Fine," Cassie grumbled. She pushed the covers away, sat up and leaned back against the headboard. Sally handed her the cup. Cassie sniffed it. *It smells like spices.* She raised the cup to her lips and took a sip. *It tastes tart, but not too bad.* She braved a few more sips and waited for her stomach to rebel. It grumbled and rumbled but the tea stayed down. *Maybe the comté does know what he is talking about.*

"Perhaps you can try some toast later." Sally placed a plate of dry toast triangles on the bedside table.

Cassie nodded; then sipped her tea thoughtfully. "I really liked being kissed by the comté. His kisses make me feel all…tingly, inside. Do you think that means I am immoral?"

Sally giggled. "Certainly not, I think you are sad and lonely. It must be awful to be married to one as old as the earl." She paused, a slight blush staining her cheeks. "I think I would fall in love with the comté, too, if I were you. He is so handsome and kind."

She shook her head, careful not to meet the maid's gaze. "I am not in love with the comté. I hardly know him, besides, like it or not, I am married to the earl."

"That does not mean you cannot be in love with someone else," Sally pointed out.

"What good does it do one to love someone you know you cannot have? I would just be torturing myself by wanting him."

"Many ladies have discreet romantic affairs whilst they are married," Sally whispered.

She choked on her tea. "That is positively scandalous, Sally! I could not go sneaking around behind my husband's back."

"Not until you have given the earl his heir, I suppose, perhaps after that he would turn a blind eye." Sally shrugged, a twinkle in her eye.

"I just could not do it. What would Papa say?"

"He would not know."

Before Cassie could think any more on the subject she heard the connecting door to the earl's bedchamber open. She waved Sally to silence and listened to the *tap tap* of his cane coming toward her room.

The earl shuffled into the bedchamber without knocking. Sally gave him a quick curtsy and hurried out. He came to stand by Cassie's bedside. "Are you feeling any better this morning?"

"No, my lord. I do not think the sea agrees with me."

"Hum," the earl said, looking closely at her, "You shall have to endure another couple days of the sea yet."

"Yes, my lord," Cassie mumbled. She traced the rim of her teacup nervously with her fingertip.

"Your maid tells me she has been teaching you to sew to pass the time."

Cassie nodded. It was best not to offer any details for she had no idea how the earl would feel about her activities.

"A lady does not sew, girl, she embroiders," he said, sounding vexed. "If you must keep yourself occupied on this trip I shall endeavor to find you some proper embroidery materials. Perhaps that will keep you out of trouble."

Cassie stifled the urge to tell him just what she thought of his ridiculous ideas. Oh, how she longed to protest his childish treatment. It would not do to prick his ire any further. Instead, she forced a stiff smile to her lips. "Thank you."

The earl nodded, gave her a smug look, and left.

She breathed a sigh of relief and leaned back against her pillows. Reaching for a toast point, she popped a bit in her mouth, chewed, and swallowed cautiously. Her stomach rolled, but the toast stayed down. With a grin she picked up the plate and made quick work of the rest of it with a mental note to send a letter of thanks to the comté for recommending the ginger root tea.

Sally came back into the room with her sewing basket. "I thought since you learned the first stitch so quickly I would teach you another today."

"The earl says a proper lady does not sew, she embroiders," Cassie mimicked, making a face.

"We shall not tell him." The maid perched on the edge of the bed and they spent the rest of the day sewing.

* * * *

Sally was settling a dinner tray across Cassie's lap when there was a knock on the sitting room door. She hurried to open it.

A young sailor stood there. "Comté Ashton bade me deliver a package to Lady Everton." He held out a small package wrapped in plain brown paper.

Sally thanked him and took the package. She shut the door and hurried to the settee where Cassie sat and handed her the gift.

"I wonder what it is." She turned the article around in her hands.

"There is only one way to find out," Sally scolded. "Open it."

Using the butter knife off her plate, Cassie carefully slit the paper.

Inside was a beautifully carved oriental box. Grasping the clasp she lifted the lid. A tiny jade elephant lay nestled in the red velvet interior. "Oh, my," Cassie breathed, picking up the delicate carving and turning it around in her hands to admire it. "It is beautiful! Have you ever seen anything so perfect?"

The maid gave her a puzzled look. "What is it?"

Cassie smiled. "It is an elephant; just like the one I saw when I boarded the ship. I wonder where it came from?"

Sally looked over her shoulder. "You best hide it somewhere so the earl does not see it."

Cassie placed the tiny figurine back in its velvet cradle and hid the box in her accessory trunk with a smile. "I suppose I must send it back to him."

"Why?" Sally frowned at her.

"I would not want the comté to think I was in favor of his pursuit. How would it look if I were to accept his gifts?" *The elephant was thoughtful...sweet even, if truth be told.* "Perhaps it would not hurt to keep the comté's present, just this once."

Chapter Eight

They had been in Bath for two whole days already and she was still sick to her stomach. How did one get seasick on land Cassie wondered bitterly?

The maid hurried into the room with a cup of ginger root tea. "We are almost out of tea, my lady."

Cassie took the steaming cup with a grateful smile and crossed to the dressing table. Sitting, she sipped while the maid styled her hair. "Perhaps you could ask at the market for someone who sells it? The earl gave me a shilling to throw into the wishing well yesterday. He told me to pray for a babe when I tossed it, but I only pretended to and pocketed the coin. It seemed like such a waste."

Sally smiled. "You are very clever." She grew serious for a moment. "When was your last monthly flow?"

She ticked off the weeks in her head. "It has been a little over four weeks now. I suppose it has been delayed because I have been ill. Why do you ask?"

The maid stared at her thoughtfully for a moment. "Is it possible your queasy stomach could be the result of already being with child?"

Cassie set her cup down abruptly, sloshing the hot tea over her hand in the process. She blew on the burned flesh to cool the pain while Sally ran to dip a cloth in the cold water from the pitcher in the bathing room. *Could I be carrying the earl's child?* She stared at her reflection in the mirror. She looked tired and drawn, attesting to the fact she was not sleeping well. *Does being with child cause one to sleep as uneasily as I have for the last few weeks?*

"I do not think it is possible," she said when Sally came back and placed the cool cloth on her scalded hand. "Morning sickness does not continue all day and into the night or they would call it day sickness."

Sally shook her head. "When my mama was carrying my brother she was sick all day."

"I suppose it is possible, but surely I would have had morning sickness weeks ago since it has been three months since the earl has visited my bed."

"I am not sure, my lady, perhaps you should have the earl summon a physician and consult him."

Cassie felt as if butterflies danced in her stomach. *Could I really be with child?* The earl would be so pleased and she would have a child to dote upon. Her excitement grew as she imagined a chubby faced child running through the quiet halls of the earl's mansion. She placed a hand on her flat stomach. *Could there be even now a tiny child growing within?*

Without waiting for Sally to finish her hair, Cassie sprang from the stool and ran in search of her husband. Flushed and breathless she almost reached the bottom of the stairs when the earl hobbled passed.

He gave her a cross look when he spotted her, his snowy white brows coming to an ominous point. "How many times must I tell you not to bound down the stairs in such an undignified manner, girl?"

She stopped and walked sedately down the remaining two steps, hard pressed to hide her grin, too happy to be brought low by his scolding. "I need to speak with you my lord, right now, if you please. It is important."

The earl scowled at her. "I am sure whatever is on your mind could have waited until you made a more ladylike decent."

"I am sorry, my lord, I was sure you would want to hear my news right away."

He snorted and shook his head. "Well, what is it then?"

Cassie paused, not sure exactly how to say what was on her mind delicately.

He frowned at her reluctance. "Spit it out, girl!"

"It has come to my attention, well, I may be with child, my lord," Cassie said hesitantly.

His eyebrows rose to attention; then he gave her a twisted grimace that might pass for a smile before bellowing, "Bernard."

The butler came on the run from down the hallway. "Yes, my lord?"

The earl tucked her hand in the crook of his arm. "Bernard, summon a physician right away so I may confirm Lady Everton's good news."

Bernard cast a doubtful look her way and hurried to do as he was bid.

The earl escorted Cassie back up the stairs. "Now tell me girl, why do you think you are with child?"

"Well, my lord, you are aware I felt poorly on the ship. However, since we have been on solid land these past two days I have felt no better. My maid claims I might have what they call morning sickness." She hugged the idea of a child tight in her heart.

The earl nodded. When they reached Cassie's room he ushered her inside. "I want Lady Everton to rest in bed until the physician gets here. Go get her a breakfast tray. She is not to be running up and down the stairs," he lectured the maid. When Sally nodded and left, the earl patted Cassie's hand. "Do as you are told like a good girl and get back into bed. I will send the physician straight up when he arrives." He favored her with another of his odd twisted smiles and left the room.

She climbed into bed and hugged herself. *Finally, I have pleased him.*

* * * *

Cassie settled back against the pillows with a joyous smile as the physician repacked his medical bag. She looked up as the earl entered the room.

"Well?" he prompted the younger man.

The doctor smiled. "Congratulations, my lord. Lady Everton is indeed with child. Everything looks just fine. She should rest, do light exercise, and get plenty of fresh air every day. If all goes well she should deliver a fine healthy infant approximately eight months from now."

The earl's smiled faded and he looked at her strangely for a moment. "Are you sure you have calculated right, young man? Is it not customary for a child to be born nine months or so after conception?"

The doctor looked puzzled for a moment. "Yes, my lord, you are quite right. Eight months from now would be February. I expect the child to arrive the last week in February. If you will excuse me now, I have another patient to attend."

The earl nodded and Bernard escorted the doctor from the room.

Cassie froze when she saw the look of contempt on the earl's face. *Oh God! The child I carry is not the earl's.* There was no other answer, and she had lain with no man except her husband, other than the night the mysterious stranger visited her bed.

"Well?" the earl snarled. "What explanation do you have for this miracle, girl? I have not lain with you these three months past and yet you are only one month pregnant."

Cassie watched in horror as the earl advanced on her in fury.

"Well?" he spat, his face turning an alarming shade of red.

She flinched and shrank back against the pillows when he slammed his cane down on the bedside table.

"Have you nothing to say?"

"I am so sorry, my lord." What could she say? The frantic beating of her heart sounded in her own mind, almost drowning out all rational thought. *There is no truth that can save me from his wrath, none that he will believe anyway, for I hardly believe it....*

"Sorry?" His face twisted into a frightening sneer as he leaned over and grabbed her by the hair. "Who have you spread your legs for, girl?"

Cassie sobbed in pain as he twisted the hair in his hand. "I do not know, my lord."

"You will tell me who the father of your bastard is so I may have the whore-son killed!"

"I do not know!" Terror clawed at her insides. What was he going to do to her?

The earl let go of her hair as if he had been burned. "I gave you my name, a title, a position higher than you could have ever hoped for and you betrayed me!" He placed a hand over his heart as if he had been mortally wounded by her unfaithful act.

"I did not mean for it to happen, my lord. It was dark and I did not see his face." Covering her face with her hands she sobbed in mortification.

"What are you talking about girl?"

Dropping her hands she took a deep wavering breath. "It

happened the night your Egyptian artifact was stolen. I awoke, and he was in my bedchamber. It was dark, and I could not see his face."

He gawked at her with an incredulous expression. "You shared your bed with a thief?"

"Please," Cassie pleaded. "Please believe me; I did not want it to happen."

"Are you telling me the thief who stole my artifact raped you? Why did you not cry for help? Why did you not tell me sooner?"

"I-I was ashamed. I was afraid to tell you," Cassie wailed, desperate for him to accept her story.

The earl stared at her for a moment. "I do not know whether to believe your tale or not. Until I decide what to do about this you will remain locked in your room."

Cassie nodded, unable to decide if she should be grateful he at least had not beaten her or cast her out of his house. The idea of being locked away was almost as frightening.

The earl left and true to his word, Cassie heard the key scrape in the lock. She tossed back the covers and wandered over to the window. From here she could see the changing huts bordering the hot springs. If she was locked in her room for the remainder of their stay she would not get to sample the waters. She had so looked forward to the experience... If her husband cast her out of his house where would she go? Her father would not welcome her home carrying a bastard in her belly. Even if she were carrying the earl's child she doubted she would be welcome when there were already so many other mouths to feed.

With no money and nowhere to go what was she to do? The comté had been so kind to her, would he help her? She decided even if he offered to help she could not bear to tell him of her scandalous behavior. The only thing left to do was throw herself on the earl's mercy. Cassie leaned her forehead against the window pane, silent tears trickling down her cheeks. Relying on her husband's mercy did not seem to be the most promising option at this moment.

She spun around when the key scraped in the lock. The door opened and Sally hurried in with a basket. Bernard shut the door behind her, the snick of the lock evidence the earl did not intend to renege on his promise.

"Why is the door locked, my lady?"

"I am not allowed to leave my room, Sally. The earl is angry with me. I am to stay locked away until he has decided what is to become of me."

Sally frowned. "Why would he be angry? If you were wrong about being with child, it was an honest mistake."

Cassie looked down at her hands as tears overcame her, rolling down her cheeks and dripping to the carpet silently. "I *am* with child, Sally. The problem is it is not the earl's."

Chapter Nine

Ashton strolled through the open market, stopping occasionally to peruse the different wares that interested him. A boy pushed past him, knocking a young woman ahead of him off balance. He caught her arm, steadying her as she bumped into him.

"I am sorry, sir." Her gaze caught his and she gaped at him. "My lord, forgive me for addressing you incorrectly."

Aston smiled and tipped his hat. "No apologies are necessary, Miss-?"

"Sally."

He nodded. "Ah, yes, Sally. You are Lady Everton's maid, are you not?"

"Yes, my lord." She nodded and lowered her head.

"How is your mistress?" He frowned when the maid's face paled at the mention of her mistress. "I trust she is feeling better now she is back on solid ground?"

"No." The maid heaved a loud sigh. "That is why I am here at the market. I was hoping to find some more ginger root tea for my lady."

"Has she seen a physician?" Ashton asked, concerned.

The maid blushed, looking at the basket she clutched in her hand. "Yes, my lord. It seems my lady is with child and suffers from morning sickness. The tea seems to help."

"I see. Well you will not find any ginger root here. It is a special root I brought back with me from my last architectural dig in China." When disappointment etched on her face he gave her a crooked grin and leaned closer. "You see, I suffer from a slight case of seasickness myself," he said in a conspiratorial tone.

"Oh." The maid's eyes grew round.

"Come with me. I have plenty more ginger root back at the town house I am renting during my stay in Bath."

"I really must be getting back." Her gaze flickered nervously around the market. "Lord Everton does not know I am out."

"My lodgings are not far from here," Ashton reassured her with a smile. "I would have a messenger send it for me, but I suspect the earl would not approve."

The girl looked crestfallen. "Yes, you are right. The earl is so very angry with my lady right now. It would not do to give him cause to punish her further."

"Come, this way then." He hurried through the mingling people back to the entrance to the market. Once they were clear of the crowd he slowed his pace so the maid could walk beside him. He glanced at her. "It is none of my business, but is the earl still angry with Lady Cassandra because of me?"

The maid paled. "No."

"Then why is he angry with her?"

She looked away. "He is angry because Lady Everton is with child."

Ashton stared at the little maid in confusion. "I am afraid I do not understand. I was under the distinct impression the earl wanted a child."

"Oh, he does. It is just that—" Her face took on a distinctly scarlet hue and she fixed her gaze on the cobblestones beneath her feet. "I really should not say, my lord, it would not be proper to gossip."

"Perhaps I could help in some way? You would not be gossiping, you would merely be asking my advice." When the girl tilted her head and lifted a brow in doubt he smiled kindly.

"I suppose I can trust you, since you have been so nice," she said hesitantly. "My poor lady does not know what to do, my lord, and I have no idea how to help her."

"Tell me the problem and perhaps we can figure out a solution between the two of us."

"It is a very delicate tale, not one meant for a man's ears," she said quietly.

"Forget for a minute I am a man. I am Lady Everton's friend who wants very much to help." They turned the street corner. "Here, come into my private parlor where you can explain the situation without fear of being overheard." He opened the door to his leased townhouse. The girl faltered before reluctantly entering. He escorted her to the parlor;

then rang for the housekeeper to bring them some tea and a packet of his special ground ginger root. "Now, explain to me Lady Cassandra's problem." He took a seat across from the maid who looked decidedly uncomfortable in the luxurious room.

"Well, my lord," the maid began, "the child my lady now carries is not the earl's."

Ashton frowned. "I see, how does she know?"

The maid blushed a deep red. "The dates do not match with the days the earl visited my lady's bed."

"Whose child is it then, if I may ask?"

"That is part of the problem, my lord." The maid wrung her hands. "She does not know."

Ashton tried to stifle his anger. He thought Lady Cassandra an innocent, but it appeared she was more experienced than he guessed. Had she sent the maid in search of him in hopes he would rescue her from her predicament because he was kind to her? Did she think him a fool? Ashton snorted. "What do you mean she does not know? She must have some idea unless she makes a habit of climbing into other men's beds on a regular basis."

"Oh no, it is not like that, my lord," the maid hurriedly assured him. "My lady was taken advantage of one night in her own bedchamber."

Ashton gave her a skeptical look. "Taken advantage of? How so?"

"It was the night of Lord Everton's dinner party. You remember the one where he displayed his Egyptian artifact?"

When Ashton nodded the maid went on with her story.

"Well, my lady never had wine before, and she did admittedly drink too much. After she retired and was fast asleep in her bed, an intruder broke into the house and stole the earl's artifact. He made his escape through my lady's bedchamber. I suppose he thought to hide out until it was quiet so he could sneak out her window, but she awoke...." the maid trailed off looking down at the carpet.

"Then what happened?"

"Well, she thought at first it was Lord Everton, as it had been a while since he visited her bedchamber. By the time my lady realized it was not he, it was too late."

The lady told her maid. Did she also tell her husband? Ashton cleared his throat. "I see. Was this rascal apprehended?"

"No, my lord, Lady Everton never told anyone save me what happened and only recently the earl."

"Why did she not cry out for help or tell her husband right away?"

"She felt guilty and embarrassed, my lord, because she admitted to me she responded to the thief's touch."

"So she is a woman of loose virtue."

"Oh, no, my lord, she is not! She feels she is to blame and is sure God is punishing her for her sin."

"I see," Ashton said slowly. "Has Lady Everton told the earl all of this?"

"Yes, but the earl does not believe her. He has locked her in her room until she identifies the thief and father of her child."

"I see," Ashton said again, pondering the situation. At least he had not beaten the poor woman. "Since she does not know who the intruder was she cannot name a man to the crime."

"Exactly." The maid looked at him beseechingly. "What is she to do, my lord?"

Ashton stood. "There does not seem to be anything, my dear, but wait to see what the earl decides to do when Lady Everton does not come up with the name he seeks. My guess is he will cover the whole matter up and accept the child as his, at least publicly."

The maid looked on the verge of panic, hers eyes wide and fearful. "What if he does not accept the child? What if he casts my lady out? She has no place to go and no skills to earn her own keep, let alone that of a babe."

"We shall just have to wait and see. I cannot interfere in the earl's marriage. If he casts Lady Everton out, bring her to me and I will see no harm befalls her." He showed the maid out with her packet of ginger root.

"Thank you, my lord."

Ashton shut the door behind her. He seriously doubted the earl's pride would allow him to claim another man's child as his own. He would have to find a way to help Lady Cassandra.

Chapter Ten

Cassie put her hand to her swollen belly and launched her considerable bulk from the chair. She crossed to the window and looked out on the winter landscape. Deep drifts turned brush and flower beds into shapeless white mounds. A few snowflakes drifted against the window pane and melted. She rubbed the small of her back where it ached increasingly each day with the growing weight of the babe.

The earl would be here soon to interrogate her, as was his nightly routine since they returned from their shortened trip to Bath. Every day he asked her to name the father of her child, and every day she told him she did not know. He kept true to his threat, and she had spent the last eight months locked in her room with only Sally for company. A beating would have been better than months of imprisonment she reflected sourly.

When the key scraped in the lock she did not turn, but remained staring out the window. The familiar *tap, tap* of the earl's cane announced his presence.

His tone was as icy as the landscape beyond the window pane. "Well, girl, what have you to say for yourself today?"

Cassie remained silent. It would do no good to tell him again she did not know the answer to his unasked question.

"Your time is almost up, girl, the child will be born any day now."

Cassie turned, glaring at him.

Venomous words dripped from his sneering lips. "Your lover is not interested in laying claim to your bastard, else he would have made his intentions known by now."

The child kicked, and Cassie rubbed her stomach gently. The earl scowled at the movement of her hand and hobbled toward her. Wrapping her arms protectively around her belly she stood defiantly waiting.

He stopped when he was within arms' reach. "I have decided to claim your bastard as mine."

She was not sure whether to be relieved or dismayed by his statement until his next words made her heart freeze.

"However, I can never forgive you for your deceitfulness. After the child is born you will leave my house. The child, of course, will remain here with me."

Cassie stared at the earl in shock, her breath squeezing against her ribcage. "I will not abandon my child!"

"You do not have any say in the matter, girl. The law is on my side, I have the right to keep the child, and there is nothing you can do about it." He sneered at her, his eyes hard and cold.

She fought to keep her growing panic in check. She must remain in control. Surely there was a way she could convince him to let her stay with her child. "Who will care for the babe if not me?"

He scoffed. "That is what a wet nurse is for, girl. No lady of quality would suckle her child at any rate, so you see, I really do not need you."

Her world came crashing down. *No! God, no!* "Please, my lord, *please* do not take my child from me! I will do anything you ask."

Turning his back on her cries he hobbled to the door.

Cassie followed him, begging him to reconsider. "Please my lord. I shall do anything you ask."

He stopped on the threshold and spat on her. "The sight of you sickens me and I will not have you taint the child with your sinful nature."

Without bothering to wipe the spittle from her cheek she grasped his arm, tears streaming down her face. "Please, do not do this!"

With a look filled with loathing he shook off her hand and walked out, slamming the door in her face. Cassie sunk to the floor and sobbed uncontrollably as the key clicked in the lock.

What am I going to do? I cannot let the earl take my child. Distress and hysteria overtook her, clouding her mind until all she knew was profound heartbreaking grief.

Bernard let Sally into the room. She knelt beside Cassie. "My lady, what is the matter? Please do not cry so, you will harm the babe."

"My babe!" Cassie wailed. "He is going to take my child, Sally!"

"Who is going to take your child?" She helped Cassie to her feet and led her over to a chair by the fire.

"The earl is going to take the babe and send me away." Cassie clung to the maid's hand in desperation. "What am I going to do?"

Sally helped Cassie lower her bulk into the chair. "I will go to Comté Ashton. He told me to send for him if you needed his help."

Cassie sniffled, trying to get control over her emotions. "When did you speak with the comté?"

"I went to the market in Bath, to look for the ginger root you needed those first months for the morning sickness. I could not find any, but I bumped into the comté there."

"He will not help a fallen woman." Cassie wanted to believe he would help her, although her hope was slim.

Sally handed her a handkerchief. "He does not think you a fallen woman. I explained to him what happened and he was most kind. He told me if the earl cast you out, to send for him at once and he would ensure you were safe."

"He said that?" Cassie sniffed and wiped her tears with the dainty handkerchief.

"Yes, he did," Sally said with a gentle smile. "After you have your dinner I shall send word to the comté, and he will come to help you."

Cassie nodded, reassured the comté would have a solution to her dilemma.

As Sally placed the dinner tray on the table beside her chair a sharp pain lanced through her lower back. She cried out.

"My lady, what is the matter?"

Cassie looked up as the pain intensified. "I think the babe is coming."

"Let me help you to bed, if the pains do not stop I will send for the physician."

Cassie nodded and allowed the maid to help her up from the chair and to the bed. Over the next few hours the pains became worse until they were hardly bearable. She writhed on the bed, struggling to breathe through the contractions. "Sally...please...do something...surely there is...a way...to make...the labor stop."

The helplessness on the maid's face mirrored Cassie's inner

turmoil. "There is naught I know of, my lady, else I would try it."

"Did you send for Comté Ashton?" Cassie moaned again, pain rippling through her.

"Yes, my lady, I did, but there is no word from him yet."

Cassie clenched the bed covers, panting until the pain subsided.

The door opened and the physician entered. "I see your time is upon you, Lady Everton." He crossed to the bed and set down his medical bag.

She did not have time to answer before another contraction was upon her. Crying out she gripped the bed posts as the physician lifted the sheet covering her legs and looked underneath.

"Get some hot water and towels ready," he told the maid. "Rest assured, Lady Everton, you shall hold your baby in your arms before the clock strikes twelve this night."

"Nooo," Cassie moaned.

"There is no need to fear, my lady, you are strong and healthy. You should deliver with no problems," he assured her, misunderstanding her protest.

Just before midnight Cassie heaved a final exhausted push and gave birth to her son. When the physician placed the swaddled infant in hers arms, she cuddled the warm bundle to her and cried with a mixture of happiness and sorrow. *I will not let him take you from me.* Nestling her chin against her child's dark hair she closed her eyes and let sleep clear her mind of worry.

* * * *

It was quiet. A dull ache between her legs reminded her of the child she labored to bring into the world. Slowly she opened her eyes to weak winter sunlight streaming in through the window. "Where is my baby?"

Sally hurried to her side with a tray of tea and toast and helped her sit up. "He is right next door with the wet nurse, my lady. He is a right handsome lad," she boasted with a bright smile.

"I would like to see him." She caught sight of the basket of baby clothes on the floor by the bed she and Sally spent the winter sewing.

Did the earl seek to remove all trace of her from the child's life?

The maid's face turned gloomy and she shook her head. "The earl has forbidden it. He said you are to leave at the end of the week. He has acquired a position of service for you at St. Catherine's Convent."

"He is sending me to a convent?" Cassie stared at her.

The maid looked down at her hands. "Yes, my lady. I am to be let go to find another position elsewhere."

Cassie pushed the tray from her lap untouched. What was she to do? The earl did not utter idle threats. She blinked back her tears and fought to keep her voice from breaking. "Have you heard from the comté yet?"

The maid shook her head and removed the tray.

"I have to get my son and find a way to escape." Cassie lifted her chin with resolve. "I will find a way."

"The door is still locked," Sally reminded her. "Even if you could get away from here where would you go, and how would you get there without coin?"

"I do not know, Sally. I do not know." The thin lifeline of hope she clung to was fading rapidly.

Sally sat on the edge of the bed, her face a mask of despair. "The earl is having a party tonight. Perhaps the comté will be there and I can ask him what to do."

"If the comté was going to help me, Sally, he would have sent word I am sure."

* * * *

Cohen stepped down from his carriage and rubbed his tired eyes. As he mounted the steps to his rented lodgings a young messenger boy hailed him from the street. He paused, despite the cold blast of wind which threatened to do away with his hat as the boy hurried to catch up.

"Lord Ashton, I have a message for you."

Cohen heaved an exasperated sigh and frowned. "Can it not wait until I have changed and shaved?"

The boy scuffed the toe of his worn boot in the skiff of snow on the bottom step. "'Tis urgent, my lord. I have been waiting all night for your return."

One look at the boy's stiff blue lips convinced Cohen the lad most likely had been there all night. "Fine, come inside where it is warmer. I have traveled through the night from my country home and want nothing more than to go to bed," he complained crossly.

Once inside he hung up his coat and called for the housekeeper. When she arrived he sent her to fetch him something to eat. He motioned for the chilled boy to follow him to the library. A fire crackled in the hearth as the odd pair stood in front of the flames and rubbed their hands.

He glanced at the boy. "Who sent you and what is your important message, lad?"

"Sally, Lady Everton's maid sent me, milord. She bade me wait and not come back until I saw you."

Cohen's heart leaped in his throat. Was Lady Everton in trouble?

The boy continued. "Sally says to tell you the babe is coming and her lady will be sent away after it is born."

"*Damn!*" The swear word slipped from his lips. When the boy looked frightened he gave him a coin and patted his arm. "Thank you, lad. On your way out stop at the kitchen and tell the housekeeper I said to find you something to eat." The boy nodded and hurried out.

Cohen paced the study floor. The law was clearly on the earl's side if he chose to cast Lady Cassandra from his door. There was no way he could convince the man to relinquish the lady's child he was sure, so what could be done?

He caught sight of an envelope on his desk, strolled over, and picked it up. It was an invitation to the unveiling of the rest of the earl's archaeological find from Egypt, tonight at seven o'clock at his London townhouse. He looked at his fob watch. It was nearly six o'clock already. If he hurried he could bath, change, and still be there on time. Maybe it was not yet too late to help Lady Cassandra.

Chapter Eleven

The clock downstairs finished chiming the three o'clock hour. Cassie rolled over and stared at the canopy above her. The glow from the firelight cast shifting shadows across the fabric, giving the illusion the material was alive and moving. She rolled back onto her side. Sleep eluded her as she worried her dilemma over and over in her mind. *What am I to do? How am I to get my son? Where will I go? If I go home to my family will they send me back to the earl?* She allowed the tears to flow as her feeling of helplessness reached its peak. *I am going to lose my son and there is nothing I can do about it. It is all my fault. I am sinful and now God is punishing me.*

Burying her head in her pillow she cried, wails of grief breaking the silence of her prison. It did not matter if anyone heard her. No one cared. The comté had not come to help her as he promised, and tomorrow she would be cast out, never to see her son again. Even if she knotted her sheets together and risked the precarious climb down from the second floor, she could not rescue her son. The door was locked. *It is hopeless. I want to die.*

At first, the flutter of the bed curtains did not register to her weary mind. Then she heard the click of the door as it shut. She willed her gasping breaths to slow so she could listen. *Perhaps my mind is playing tricks.* The soft rustle of material made her sit up. The drapes that kept the drafts from the bed shifted slightly.

"Sally?" Her whisper broke the quiet like a shout. Heart pounding, she froze, clutching the bed clothes to her breast. *Someone is in the room.*

The curtain slid back ever so slowly. She searched the darkness for the cause of their movement. A dark figure stepped to the side of the bed and she drew back in alarm. Before she could cry out, her mouth was covered with a hand.

"Hush."

She tried to pull the hand away and scramble from the bed, but before she could gain her freedom, the mattress dipped and she found herself pinned under the intruder's weight.

The familiar voice whispered again. "Hush."

Cassie stilled, trying to place him.

"I mean you no harm. I am here to help you. I will take my hand off your mouth if you promise not to scream."

A strangely familiar scent tickled her nostrils when she drew a deep breath in through her nose. *That cologne. I have smelled it before. When?* Recognition dawned in her mind. *It is him!* She nodded slowly to be sure he understood and he released his hand. "You!" she hissed. "What are you doing here?"

The figure shifted slightly. "Hush."

"Go away, thief! You have already caused me enough trouble!"

"Where is the babe?"

She glared at him, suspicion filling her. "He is not with me, why?"

His breath of wonder hung between them. "He? I have a son."

"Why?" she repeated, louder this time.

"Be quiet," he reprimanded her. "I have come for my son."

He must have heard her sharp intake of breath as she prepared to scream because he clapped his hand back over her mouth. "For God's sake, do not scream!" the words hissed between his teeth. "If you want to get out of here, pack some things quickly, and be ready to go when I get back." When she nodded he lifted his hand from her mouth again.

"Why should I trust you?"

He brushed an errant curl from her face. "What other choice do you have?"

She studied his shadowed face for a moment. *He is right, what other choice do I have? The comté is not coming. I have to trust the thief, at least until I am away from the earl. Then I will figure out what to do.*

"Well?"

The impatience in his tone had her scrambling from the bed.

"Where is the baby?"

"He is locked in the next room."

"Get a few things packed by the time I get back." Without waiting for a reply he slipped back under the curtain.

Cassie hurried to pack as much as she could into an empty pillowcase. Something, not a sound really but more of a feeling, made her look up. She gasped and jumped when she spied him standing there watching her.

He crossed to the bed and laid a bundle on it. "Do you have a shawl?"

She picked up a white shawl from the pile at her feet and handed it to him. He fashioned it into a sling which he tied across his chest. Taking the bundle he slid it into the sling. When it gurgled she realized he had found the baby.

"Are you ready?"

When she nodded he reached into a sack on the floor and took out a rope with a small grapple attached. He crossed to the window and opened it. After he secured the grapple to his satisfaction he motioned for her to climb over the sill.

"I cannot climb down there!" she whispered with a terrified shake of her head.

"Then you stay here."

The finality of his words propelled her to snatch up her sack and hurry to his side. Leaning forward she looked out the window. It was a long way to the ground. At her hesitation, he took the pillowcase, tied it to his belt, and pulled her roughly to him. A terrified squeal slipped unbidden from her lips, and she wrapped her arms around his neck as he swung his legs over the windowsill. She could see his teeth gleaming as he grinned, easing their weight onto the rope. Her breath caught as he ever so slowly let the rope slide through his hands, wrapping it around his leg to slow their decent. She felt his chest vibrate against her cheek and realized he was enjoying her distress. He grunted when they slid suddenly toward the ground two stories below before he regained control. With a startled squeak she wrapped her legs around his hips.

"Damn it! I cannot control our descent with your legs clamped around me," he growled in her ear.

"We are going to fall!" She clung tighter to him.

He grunted. "If you do not quit rubbing your lovely body against mine in such a suggestive way we *will* fall."

Cassie closed her eyes and reluctantly let her legs dangle, ignoring his amusement as they resumed their careful descent. His shirt grew warm and damp against her cheek, his arms shaking with the strain of his effort. Finally when she feared he could not hold their weight any longer, their feet touched the ground. He let go of the rope and gently disengaged her arms from around his neck, laughing softly at her audible sigh of relief. A practiced flick of his wrist disengaged the grapple, and he returned it to his satchel.

He leaned against the wall for a minute, his harsh breathing the only noise. "This way," he whispered, catching his breath. Grasping her hand he pulled her along behind him, keeping to the wall to stay clear of the worst of the snow drifts. By the time they reached the path leading from the servant's entrance to the back gates her feet were sodden and cold in her delicate slippers.

After easing the gate open, he paused for a moment to listen. Somewhere down the street a dog barked. He drew her along behind him, slipping through the gate and making his way to a horse tied in the alley. The animal turned its head and nickered as they approached.

Cassie hung back. "I do not know how to ride," she whispered, knowing the tremble in her voice betrayed her fear.

"You ride or you walk. We have a long way to go tonight," he whispered back.

Taking a deep breath she reached for the saddle and placed her foot in his cupped hand. He helped her up onto the horse and handed the baby to her, securing the sling around her. After tying their bundles to the saddle he mounted behind her.

It began to snow in earnest as he reached forward, took up the reins in one hand and turned the horse onto the road. With a soft cluck he nudged the animal into a slow trot.

The bouncing caused the baby to fuss. Within minutes he began to wail in earnest, his cries echoing through the empty streets.

"Hush him up," the man hissed in her ear.

Cassie anxiously shifted the baby who continued to cry.

"For God's sake, feed him!"

"I cannot."

"Here." He reached around with his free hand and loosened her cloak. Then he slipped his cool hand underneath and unfastened the top four buttons on the back of her gown.

Cassie tried to wiggle away. "Stop, what are you doing?"

He pushed the gown off her shoulders to free her breasts. "I am trying to help you. Now be quiet." Pulling her against him, he pulled down the top of her chemise and shifted the child to her breast. She tensed as he lifted her tender, engorged breast to the baby. Her son smacked his lips and latched onto her nipple. Cassie clenched her teeth as the action caused her breast to throb painfully.

The man kept his hand there to support her as the horse jogged down the darkened streets. The baby alternated between making sucking sounds and whimpering fretfully. When she could no longer bear the pain, she began to cry. Sobs racked her body, tears rolling down her cheeks.

"Bloody hell, I am only trying to help you feed the boy!"

She hiccoughed. "It is not that."

"Then why is it you cry?" he asked, irritation straining his words.

"It hurts, and I-I do not think he is getting anything," she whimpered.

He moved his hand, and she steeled herself against his seeking fingers as he felt her hot, tender breast.

"Have you fed the child before now?"

"No."

"You are too full for him to suckle properly. Hold on." He nudged the horse into an easy canter, his hand still cupping her. She peered through the dark, trying to keep her mind off the proximity of his fingers. They turned down another street and stopped in front of a livery stable.

"Wait here." He leaped from the horse and hurried inside.

Cassie shifted in the saddle and put the baby to her shoulder to try and comfort him. A few moments later the man came back out. He helped her down from the horse and took the howling baby from her so she could hold her cloak closed. He slung the makeshift sling across his chest and bounced the child gently to comfort him as he untied their bags from the saddle.

A sleepy young boy hurried from the stable and took the horse inside as a closed coach pulled by four horses was driven from around back of the building. It stopped beside them, the driver jumping down to take the bags and open the door. When Cassandra was seated, the man climbed aboard, and settled opposite her. The coach lurched into motion. He leaned forward in his seat and pulled a water bottle from his coat. "Open your cloak and slide your dress off your shoulders."

"I beg your pardon?"

"Just do it before the child wakes up the entire city!"

While she adjusted her dress he leaned over and lit the oil lamp, turned it down low, and then hung it in the bracket on the wall. He turned toward her, the glow chasing the shadows from his face.

She gasped, staring at him dazed and confused. "Lord Ashton? I thought you were the thief."

He nodded and handed her the baby. "I am. Suckle him while I hold this warm water bottle against your breast. It will help the milk flow."

"I-I can do it myself," Cassie stammered, fumbling with the crying baby.

He switched seats to sit beside her. "No, you cannot."

He placed the water bottle against her breast as the baby smacked his lips and fussed at her nipple. With a gentle touch he stroked her hard breast until milk began to flow and the baby latched on to suckle in earnest.

Cassie tried to relax as the tightness lessened but the comté's fingers on her flesh made it difficult. She trembled despite her efforts to keep from moving. When the baby sighed in contentment he pulled her cloak around her to keep out the chill and slid back into the other seat. He added a couple of pieces of coal to the brazier on the floor and placed the water bottle beside it to keep warm. Straightening with a pleased look, he leaned back in his seat to watch her. "Is that better?"

Despite her embarrassment she nodded.

"You had better switch him to the other breast before he falls asleep or it will be worse than the first by next feeding."

Cassie tickled the baby's chin until he unlatched and switched him to the other breast which was leaking all over her chemise. She fixated on the baby, afraid to look up and unsure of what to say. She should thank him for coming to her rescue. On the other hand, it was his fault she was in this mess in the first place, was it not? He referred to the baby as his. If that were true, then he was the thief who stole the earl's artifact and the one who…who what? He had not forced himself on her exactly and she did enjoy the encounter. *Oh good Lord!* She was so tired and confused. She peeked at the comté from underneath her lashes.

His muscular legs were stretched out in front of him, crossed at the ankles, his arms folded across his chest, chin touching the black collar of his coat. His eyes were closed and she realized he was snoring softly.

She settled in the seat and closed her eyes, leaving the baby asleep at her breast. She had no idea of their destination and, in truth, it did not matter so long as she was with her son. Tomorrow she would figure things out.

Chapter Twelve

Cassie became aware of the bouncing rattle of the coach and opened her eyes. The lamp on the floor was extinguished and daylight brightened the interior. Sometime during the night she laid down across the bench and someone covered her with her cloak. The comté sat opposite her, rocking the baby in his arms. She could not help but smile as he gazed down adoringly at the little bundle.

He glanced up, caught her watching him and frowned. "You do not happen to have a change of swaddling do you? He is wet and hungry again."

She sat up and rummaged around in the pillow case until she found the swaddling clothes and one of the outfits she and Sally sewed for the baby.

The comté handed him to her. The baby began to whimper as soon as she took him in her arms. By the time she had him changed and wrapped him in a dry blanket he was wailing fitfully, his tiny fists balled tight, his face red. Before she could get the child to her breast the front of her dress was damp with milk.

The comté smiled at her frustration. "We can stop at the next town to eat, and I shall see if I can find a wet nurse."

Cassie shook her head. "I am fine."

He gave her a look that clearly said he thought she was anything but fine. "You cannot go around leaking milk all over the front of your gowns."

She blushed, pulling the cloak around her to allow her some modesty. They sat in silence for a few moments. "Where are we going, my lord?"

"We are going to Bristol, my ship is docked there. In a few weeks the ice will be thawed enough for us to sail on to Bordeaux, France, and then travel cross country to Marseilles. My home is there." He paused; then added, "My name is Cohen, by the way."

Cassie nodded, switching the baby to her other breast.

"Have you a name for our son?"

She shook her head. "He was born just prior to midnight the night before last. The earl took him away before I had a chance to name him."

"As his sire I claim the task of naming him. I have always thought to name my first born Lucca after the town in Italy where I made my first archaeological dig." He nodded as if pleased. "Does the name suit you, Cassandra?"

"Cassie," she corrected. "Yes, I like the name Lucca."

"Good, then Lucca it is."

He looked out the window until Cassie was done feeding Lucca. When she would have put the child to her shoulder to burp him Cohen reached over and took him. He put the baby to his own shoulder and gently patted his back.

"We are almost at Newbury so you might want to take the opportunity to change your dress."

She gaped at him. "You expect me to change here? In the coach?"

He shrugged, continuing to pat the baby's back. "Where else are you going to change? I could have the coachman stop so you could dress in a snow bank."

"I cannot disrobe in front of you!"

He shot her an annoyed look as the baby burped and gurgled contently. "I have made love to you and held a hot water bottle to your delightful breasts, Cassie. There is not much left for me to ogle," he assured her with a bold grin.

Cassie bit her lip and crossed her arms across her breasts to hold the loose top of her gown in place. "It is not decent, my lord, even my husband has not seen me unclothed."

"Cohen," he corrected her, "and I am not your husband."

"We could stop at an inn in the next town. Surely they will have a room where I can change."

"We do not have time to stop at an inn if we are to make Bristol before sunset. We are simply going to get fresh horses."

"Surely there is enough time for me to change whilst we wait for the horses to be switched." She held her ground stubbornly.

The corner of his lip twitched, but his face remained blank. "The less attention we draw, the better. The earl will have men scouring all of London by now looking for you and believe me when I tell you, it will not take them long to pick up our trail."

Cassie recognized the truth in his words. "You admit Lucca is your son so what could the earl do if he caught us?"

"I would not want to put you through the humiliation of a public enquiry, if in fact the earl lets it go that far, which I doubt. There is still the fact you are married to him. England does not look kindly on one who steals another man's wife. You are his property, which by law he is entitled to do with as he sees fit."

"You did not steal me from him, you rescued me." Her irritation began to grow. "Besides, the earl does not even want me."

"Call it what you will, Cassie, but the truth remains I took you from him the same as I took his Egyptian cat and his ancient tablet. He may not want you, but he does not want to lose you to the likes of me. He would kill us both first."

She gasped in horror. "Surely he would not resort murder, he would spend the rest of his days in prison."

Cohen shook his head with a grim look. "You are too naive. He would have us both killed in a heartbeat and make it look like an accident to cover his crime."

Cassie shuddered at the gruesome thought. "So what do we do? Spend the rest of our days running and hiding?"

"I have left a number of false trails for the earl's men to follow. By the time he realizes we are not in England we will be safely in France where I can deal with him on my own terms."

"Are you so sure he will know it was you who stole from him?"

"It will not take him long to figure out I took his artifacts. He will know I have you." Cohen laid the now sleeping baby on the bench beside him, and then looked out the window. "You have only a few minutes to change, Cassie."

Cassie rummaged through her sack for another chemise and dress. When she found what she was looking for she set the articles down on the bench beside her. Using her cloak for privacy she tried to shrug out of the soiled gown, but soon realized she needed to undo all of the buttons down the back in order to slip out of it. She looked up, frustrated, to see Cohen watching her with a bemused grin on his face.

"Perhaps I can help."

She hesitated. She certainly did not trust him anymore than she trusted her own body's response to his touch. Since she did not have a maid, the only options were to allow him to help her or tear her dress. The dress she might need, since there was only room for a couple in the sack.

Giving him a warning look she slipped off her cloak. Clutching her sagging bodice, she turned her back to him. The seat springs creaked. She sucked in a deep breath as his fingertips brushed her bare skin, sending little shivers through her. He worked the last button free, and she felt his breath on the back of her neck. His lips brushed the sensitive spot between her shoulder blades. Before she could protest he returned to the opposite bench.

She kept her back to him and reached for her cloak. After she pulled it shut and tied it securely she turned around. Cohen was sitting in his seat, watching her under half closed lids. She glared at him; then shrugged out of the dress, letting it fall to the floor. A little more wiggling and her chemise followed the dress. Still clutching the front of her cloak, she reached out and snatched up the clean chemise. Trying to keep the cloak closed and get the garment over her head and arms proved to be a challenge she was not prepared for.

"Could you at least close your eyes?" she complained bitterly.

He gave her a mischievous grin. "It would be easier if you would let go of the cloak."

With a snort, she stood up in the swaying coach, and turned her back on him so she did not have to worry about the cloak staying closed. At that moment they hit a pothole in the road and she was flung backward. She landed face up across Cohen's lap, her cloak gaping open to expose her nakedness underneath.

Wrapping his arm around her to keep her from tumbling to the floor, he chuckled. "See?"

When Cassie blushed and tried to scramble from his lap he held her in place. She watched, mesmerised by his brilliant green orbs as they traveled downwards to take in her exposed flesh. His eyes darkened, and his tongue slid along his bottom lip to moisten it as he trailed the fingers of his free hand down her neck to cup a full breast. Before she could glean his intent he dipped his head and kissed her. Cassie moaned as his lips brushed hers lightly; then pressed more urgently against them. He nipped her bottom lip, and she opened for him. With a groan he deepened his kiss. Her heart began to pound in her ears, her body turning to mush as he touched his tongue to hers. Suddenly he pulled away.

Cassie blinked, realising the coach had slowed.

Cohen's voice was husky and thick as he untied the laces on her cloak. "You better get dressed."

Cassie scrambled to her feet as he whipped off her cloak and held it in front of her. She shrugged into her chemise and snatched the dress from the bench, tossing it over her head. *Good Lord! The man must think I am a harlot.* Yanking the dress down, she shoved her arms into the sleeves, and looked out the window. The horses pulled up in front of a shabby livery stable. Cohen tossed her cloak onto the seat and motioned for her to turn around so he could fasten the row of tiny buttons down the back of the pale, mauve water silk gown. She turned her back to him.

"Do you have any cloth to put in your bodice?"

Cassie frowned at his familiarity. "I do not think any will fit." She looked down at the material stretching tautly across her chest. "I seem to have outgrown my clothes."

"I remember my sister having a similar problem after her first child was born." Cohen chuckled as he finished with the buttons, and then gave her a gentle push toward her seat.

She slipped her cloak back on and sat down.

Cohen handed her the sleeping baby and added a couple pieces of coal to the brazier. When the coach came to a halt he opened the door without waiting for the coachman. "Wait here." He climbed down and crossed the muddy stable yard to the barn.

Cassie watched him, admiring the way he covered the ground with long confident strides. He was always in control of the situation whereas she floundered dismally in his presence. She supposed when one was born with money and a title they naturally acquired confidence. They could buy a solution to most any situation. *Well, any dilemma except this one it seemed.*

Cuddling her son she watched as their team of muddy, sweaty horses were lead away and another team of fresh prancing ones were hitched to the coach in their place. Cohen entered her field of vision, making his way across the yard, carrying two large baskets. When he reached the coach, the driver opened the door for him and he climbed in.

The first basket he placed at Cassie's feet. It was empty except for a fluffy blue blanket. "I thought Lucca would be safer in a basket," he said at her questioning look, "that way we will not have to worry about him falling from the seat when you sleep."

"Good idea." Cassie smiled and laid the baby inside.

Cohen sat across from her and set the second basket down at his feet when the driver shut the coach door behind him. "I got something for us to eat."

Her stomach rumbled. "I am famished."

When the coach rattled forward Cohen opened the basket. He passed her a napkin on which he placed a still warm biscuit, a slice of cheese, and a thick slice of ham. Cassie made a sandwich and munched contently. "It is not the fanciest of fares, but it should tide us over for now." With a smile he followed suit, making a sandwich for himself.

When she finished eating he passed her a water skin. She pulled the cork and lifted it to her mouth, choking on the first mouthful when she realized it was wine instead of water. He grinned and passed her his handkerchief.

The baby whimpered, and Cohen nudged the basket with his boot to set it rocking gently on its rounded bottom.

Cassie wiped her mouth and handed the water skin back to him. "How is it you know so much about babies?"

He made himself another sandwich before he answered her. "I have three younger sisters and an older one. Three of them are married with seven children between them. The youngest, Emily, has always been sickly so she never married. My sisters, myself, and my older brother all live together on a winery, our main estate *Le Montennee*, just outside of Marseilles. There are always babies around it seems."

"So you have spent a lot of time around your nieces and nephews then?"

"Yes, the house is never quiet." He smiled. "I like the noise and commotion, without it a house as large as ours would be like a giant crypt."

Cassie nodded in understanding. "I always felt the same way at the earl's. Everything was always quiet; he hated noise. Makes me wonder why he even wanted children, besides needing an heir, that is. I suppose those of us who grow up in large families find the noise and energy familiar and comforting."

Cohen nodded and finished the last bite of his sandwich. He took a deep drink from the water skin and set it back in the basket at his feet. "How is it you have no baby experience since you have such a large family?"

"As the oldest I helped my father and mother minister to the poor and the sick. Every day we walked or drove our little dog cart and handed out food and clothing to those in need. My mother often nursed the sick long into the night. My sister Beth looked after the little ones mostly."

Cassie fell silent. It appeared she had more in common with Cohen than she suspected. He was so easy to talk to. Unlike the earl who did not want to know anything about her, Cohen seemed interested in her. Perhaps she was wrong, and like her husband he was really only interested in her body, she thought, recalling his earlier kiss.

Chapter Thirteen

The setting sun was painting the sky with orange and pink hues when they pulled up at the docks on the outskirts of Bristol. The small seaside town bustled with activity.

Vendors loaded their carts and shopkeepers hurried from their stores, perhaps heading home for the night, she mused. She looked out the window on the other side of the coach. Various ships floated silently on small open patches of water like the abandoned shells of memories. Cohen pointed out a large schooner anchored at the far end of the dock. "That is my ship, *Discovery*."

The coachman opened the door and Cohen tucked a blanket securely over the basket, holding the baby to keep out the draft. "Wait here."

Cassie watched him cross to the gangplank and speak to a young man in a uniform. The two men shook hands, and Cohen said something Cassie could not hear. The man answered and looked at the coach. The two men talked for a few more minutes. Cohen turned and made his way toward the coach, opened the door, and hoisted the basket from the floor. Holding out his hand, he helped her climb down, and led the way across the docks and up the gangplank.

A large man in uniform greeted them, "Good evening, Comté Ashton."

"Good evening, Rennie," Cohen responded, shaking the man's hand. "Has my cabin been aired out?"

"*Oui*, Comté."

"Good." Cohen nodded. "Come Cassie, I will show you to my quarters where you may wait while I run a few errands."

Cassie followed as he strolled across the ship's deck. They walked down a long passageway until they came to a set of double doors which a uniformed sailor stationed there opened for them. Cohen ushered her into the room ahead of him. She paused, wide eyed, on the threshold of a large parlor. The room was by far more elegant than the earl's townhouse. A gold velvet settee and two matching chairs were arranged in the corner of the room by a fancy iron brazier glowing with live coals. A large dining table was set in the other corner with chairs for ten guests and above the table a large sparkling crystal chandelier hung. Thick red and gold Persian throw rugs covered the polished wooden floor. Cassie wandered over to a painting on the wall. The man in the portrait looked down on her with a regal smile.

"His Majesty, the Emperor of France, gifted me with this ship," Cohen explained. "I was very honored, not many Englishmen are so well respected by the French monarchy."

She frowned in puzzlement. "You are English? Comté is a French title, so I thought you were French."

He nodded. "Most make that mistake. I am English born, but a titled French citizen as well."

"How is that possible?"

"Many French titles are not inherited, but bestowed upon those who earn them. My father was a poor English cloth merchant. I sailed to France and earned a title by service to the Emperor along with some wealth. After, I sent for my family and brought them to live in France. I have no noble blood, which is one of the reasons the earl dislikes me."

"Oh," was all Cassie could think of to say. Cohen was as common as she. Perhaps that was why she liked him so much from the start.

"Come, my bedchamber is this way." He gestured to an open door to the left of the dining table.

Cassie followed him to the door and stopped on the threshold. A huge bed took up most of the space in the room. It was larger by far than the bed she occupied at the earl's. It was covered with red satin and dotted with matching pillows. Did Cohen expect her to sleep with him? She swallowed.

He seemed not to notice her discomfort. "I will have one of Rennie's men bring you a bath."

Cassie nodded and Cohen left. Once the door closed behind him she went to the wardrobe to hang up her few gowns. When she opened the doors, Cohen's familiar spicy sent drifted out. His expertly tailored clothes hung neatly in rows. Did he intend to share the room with her or would he move his attire elsewhere? She pushed them closer together and hung her garments in the cleared space.

The baby began to fuss in the other room, and Cassie hurried to pick him up before his fussing turned to wailing. The baby sucked hungrily on his fist, making loud slurping noises. She set him back in the basket and reached behind her neck to undo the buttons of her dress so she could feed him. She managed the first two buttons, but could not reach the ones between her shoulder blades. Picking up the baby again she went to the door. When she opened it and looked out into the corridor, the sailor she had seen earlier was still stationed by the door, the comté was nowhere in sight.

"Do you know where Comté Ashton is?"

The man looked at her. "*Pardon Mademoiselle?*"

"The comté?" She tried again, realising he did not speak English.

The man shook his head and said something in French Cassie did not understand. She shut the door. Now what was she going to do? There was no way she could undo the buttons down the back of her dress to nurse Lucca without assistance, and there was no way she wanted to ask a stranger to help her. She put the baby to her shoulder and patted his back, trying to calm him.

Two men entered the room carrying a brass tub large enough to sit in. They set it down in front of the fire and left, returning with buckets of hot water. Cassie tried to ask them if they knew where the comté was, but neither of them spoke English. The baby began to get more upset, his whimpers turning into fitful wails.

Cassie was near tears when Cohen finally entered the parlor almost an hour later.

He looked surprised to see her pacing the room, trying to calm the screaming baby. "Why do you not feed him?"

Cassie glared at him. "I could not get my gown undone because the buttons are down the back and I cannot reach them!"

He shut the door behind him and put the packages he carried on the table.

"You left me here alone...and no one speaks English...and I could not ask anyone for help," Cassie rambled, tears rapidly spilling down her cheeks. Why was she crying? She was angry, not sad. Perhaps she was simply overtired.

Turning her around gently he made quick work of the buttons and watched over her shoulder as she lowered the baby to her breast. When the baby was suckling contently he led her to the settee to sit down. "I am sorry. I did not stop to think you might need me while I was gone."

He crossed to the table and opened the packages "I could not find a wet nurse in the village, but I did find you some pheasant blouses that lace up in the front. I also purchased a few skirts to go with them. I have some bolts of material in the ship's hold you may use if there is anything you need I have neglected to purchase. You did mention you sew." He pivoted and held up a padded chemise. "I also bought one of these," he gave her a sheepish grin. "One of the seamstresses recently had a child and said she uses one of these with pieces of cotton in the breast panels to, ah, absorb any leakage."

Cassie started to giggle but before she knew what was happening the laughter turned to sobs.

He frowned examining the undergarment. "I do not think it looks that bad."

She cried even harder as he crossed to the settee and knelt down in front of her. "I tried to find a wet nurse, but none would leave England."

Cassie shook her head. "It is not that."

"Then what is the cause of your distress?" Concern softened his gaze.

She took a shaky breath. "You have been so kind to me when you do not have to be."

Cohen smiled and brushed a stray tendril of hair from her face with gentle fingers. "It is my fault we are in this mess, and I can do no less than my best for my son."

She sniffed and wiped her eyes with the handkerchief he handed her.

He took the baby from her when he was done nursing and put him to his shoulder to burp. "Go and have your bath before the water gets cold, I will see to Lucca." He stood and picked up the packages from the table. He carried them and the baby to the bedchamber, closing the door behind them.

Cassie slipped off her dress and undergarments. She tested the water in the tub. It was still warm. With a grateful sigh she stepped in and sank in the waist deep water.

Leaning back she rested her head and closed her eyes. The warm water soothed her muscles, cramped from sitting in the close confines of the coach. Cassie realized with a start she had not asked what Cohen was going to do about the earl. *Does he have a plan? Will his family accept me, knowing I am a fallen woman? Perhaps the comté possesses the power to take Lucca away from me once we are on French soil. What will I do then? I do not even speak French. Have I made a huge mistake in trusting him? He did not mention anything about protecting me, only that he would do anything for his son. Is he only keeping me around to nourish the baby until he can find a wet nurse?*

"I brought you a towel."

Cassie sat up with a start and covered her breasts. Cohen stood beside the tub barefoot, holding out a towel. She had been so absorbed in her thoughts she did not hear him enter the room and cross the carpet.

"I would not mind bathing before the water is ice cold." He gave her an annoyed look.

She snatched the towel from him. "You could give me some privacy."

He shrugged and stripped off his shirt. "I do not see why, since I have already seen what you have to offer."

Cassie scrambled from the tub as he tossed the shirt to the floor and began to peel off his black breeches. His laughter rang in her ears as she bolted for the bedchamber before he became totally naked.

She checked on the baby. He was sleeping soundly in the middle of the big bed. Satisfied he would sleep for a while longer she changed into the new clothing. She decided to leave off her corset so she would not have to ask Cohen to lace it up for her and sat at the dressing table to brush her hair. She could not help but listen to the sounds as he splashed in the tub. The idea he was so comfortable shedding his clothes in front of her made her blush. *What would his body look like?* The earl always wore a nightshirt to bed so she did not even have him to physically compare the comté to. She tried to remember the feel of the man who made love to her in the dark, but failed. Her body had been too alive to make note of anything but what his touch did to her. Silence in the outer room told her the man was finished bathing. She hastily began to braid her hair.

Cohen padded into the room, naked except for a towel wrapped around his waist. She watched out of the corner of her eye as he crossed the room and opened the wardrobe. Muscles rippled smoothly under his taunt sun bronzed flesh, with little or no hair to mar the beauty of him. *He has the body of a god.* He pulled out clean trousers, shirt, and a waistcoat. Before he had a chance to drop the towel from his waist, Cassie removed herself from the room.

There was a tap on the door, and Cohen called out from the bedchamber, "*Entrée.*"

The sailor she saw Cohen talking to earlier entered with a tray. He nodded and smiled at her, and then crossed to the table. He took the lid off the tray and set out a meal of sausage pastries, steaming soup, sliced beef, and baby potatoes. With another nod and smile he produced a bottle of wine from his sleeve which he set on the table before leaving.

Cohen strolled into the room dressed in clean trousers, a white shirt open at the throat, and soft brown slippers. He rubbed his hair with a towel as he crossed to the table. "Ah, I see dinner has arrived. I am famished." With an easy grin he ran a hand through his tousled hair and flipped the towel over the back of the nearest chair.

Cassie held back the wistful sigh threatening to escape her lips. *He is so handsome and at ease.*

He filled a plate with a little of each food and handed it to her. After loading up his own plate he took it, and the bottle of wine, to one of the chairs by the coal brazier. Cassie sat opposite him as he poured two glasses of wine, passing one to her. He lifted his in salute. "Here is to a most lucrative burglary."

Cassie raised an eyebrow. "Burglary?"

He took a sip from his glass, grinning at her over the rim. "Yes. In addition to stealing away you and my son, I also acquired the earl's one of a kind Egyptian tablet."

"Oh." Cassie set her wine glass on the table beside her chair and concentrated on her meal. *He is too pleased with himself. Arrogant is the word for it....*

* * * *

Cassie's head drooped to her chest. With a jolt, she sat up straighter; then blinked, looking at the clock. It was past ten.

"Why do you not go to bed?" Cohen asked.

Cassie shook her head and nudged the basket containing the sleeping baby with the toe of her slipper to set it rocking.

Cohen sighed and set his book down. "Go to bed."

"Where will you sleep?"

He stood. "I will sleep in my bed as usual."

Cassie crossed her arms over her chest and glared up at him. "I am not tired."

His eyes snapped with irritation. "For God's sake Cassandra, you are falling asleep in your chair!"

"It is not proper to share a bed."

"It is not like we have not shared a bed before."

Cassie's face burned with embarrassment. "That was different. I did not know it was you in my bed, nor did I invite you in."

Cohen gave a snort of disbelief. "Like hell you did not, Cassie. Admit it, you knew I was not your soft pathetic husband the moment I touched you."

She shook her head stubbornly and refused to meet his eyes, lest he see the truth.

"Liar, your response to my touch was clear. You may lie with your lips, Cassie, but your sweet body will not deny the truth we both know."

"Must you torment me by throwing my disgraceful lack of morals in my face? Go away, and leave me be!" She turned her heat swamped face away and stared into the fire's flames.

"Come to bed."

"No. Unless you find another bed to occupy for the night."

Anger sharpened his voice. "There is no other bed. Would you have me oust my Captain from his bed instead?" He softened his tone. "Cassie, the bed is large enough for a dozen to fit. I promise I will be on my best behavior and stay on my side."

Cassie glared at him. "Do you expect me to take the word of a thief?" She was instantly sorry she uttered the comment when hurt flashed across his face only to be replaced by one of stiff anger.

"Suit yourself." He turned and stalked through the open bedroom door. It closed behind him with a resounding bang.

She sighed and got up. He had been so kind to her and in return she hit him with an unfair blow. Would he accept her apology if she were to offer it? She crossed to the bedroom door and rested her hand on the cool knob. "Cohen?" she called softly. When she received no answer she started to turn away, jumping when the door was flung open.

Cohen, shirtless, stood in the doorway, his eyes smoldering with anger. "What?"

Her courage rapidly fleeing, she swallowed. "I just wanted..." She stilled as the baby started to fuss in his basket.

"Well?" He raised an eyebrow.

"I just wanted a blanket," she finished lamely. Retreating, she hurried to pick up the baby. Sitting in the chair closest to the brazier she unlaced her blouse and put Lucca to her breast, listening to Cohen's footsteps as he crossed the room. Keeping her eyes on the baby she pretended not to hear his approach. He draped the blanket over her chair and dropped a pillow on the floor beside her. Without a word he stalked away, entered the bedchamber, and closed the door.

It appeared he would be angry with her for a while. Perhaps it was better this way. If he remained angry it was unlikely he would make any advances toward her. On the other hand, he might take his anger out on her by taking her son away when they reached France. Cassie stroked the baby's soft cheek. *I will not let him or anyone take you from me as long as I breathe.*

Chapter Fourteen

Cassie shifted on the settee, the seagulls squawking outside disturbing her rest. Stretching, she opened her eyes, blinking at the sunlight filtering in through the window. Lucca would need feeding soon. She glanced down at the basket. It was empty. Scrambling to her feet she hurried to the open bedchamber door and looked around the room. The bed was rumpled but unoccupied. Panic rose in her, wild and consuming. *Where are Cohen and Lucca?* Had Cohen taken the baby and snuck away? Terror engulfed her. *How could I be so blind and trusting? He waited until I was asleep then stole Lucca out from under my very nose!* She ran to the closet, stripped off her nightdress and pulled out a clean set of clothes. Yanking them on, she hurried to the door and flung it open. She darted into the empty corridor, fastening the laces on her blouse at the same time.

Blindly she ran down the passageway, up the stairs, and onto the deck. A sailor gave her a smile as she crossed to the gangplank.

She turned on the man. "Where is Comté Ashton?"

The man smiled and shook his head.

"The comté." Cassie screeched; her fear threatening to undo the careful stitching of her mind.

"Cassie? What is the matter?"

She spun around at the sound of Cohen's voice. "How dare you!"

Cohen gently patted Lucca's back as he held the baby against his shoulder. His brows arched with confusion. "How dare I what?"

"You cannot take Lucca! I will not let you take him from me!" Cassie flung herself at him, ready to rip him to shreds in order to retrieve her son.

He held up a hand. "What are you talking about? I simply took the child out with me so you could get some extra sleep."

Cassie's anger deflated as she stood there on the deck amid the crew's curious stares. "You took him for a walk?"

He nodded.

She sobbed, gulping for air as relief washed over her.

Cohen wrapped his free arm around her shoulders. "Cassie, did you think I took Lucca from you?"

Cassie nodded through her tears. Of course, she had; but she was wrong about Cohen, again.

He gave her shoulders a gentle squeeze. "Cass, I would never try to take our son from you. I am not a monster like Everton." He looked over his shoulder at the sailor who stood mouth agape watching them. "Come on; we better go back down to my cabin. You must be freezing without any shoes or cloak."

She looked wordlessly down at her bare feet which were already turning red with cold.

Cohen steered her to the corridor and down the passageway. Once inside, he set Lucca down in his basket and pulled Cassie into his arms.

She leaned into the warmth of his chest and breathed in his spicy scent, needing his comfort.

"I am sorry. I did not mean to frighten you." He lifted her chin to look her in the eye, his gaze searching hers. The hurt in his expression disarmed her. "Please believe me when I say I would never seek to take Lucca from you. I may be a thief, but I am not heartless."

Cassie nodded, his earnest gaze convincing her of his sincerity. "I am sorry."

The baby began to fuss. "Sit down and feed our son while I go find us something to eat." He released her, gently forcing her into the chair nearest the warm brazier. Before leaving, he placed the baby in her arms and covered them with the blanket.

Wiping her eyes on her sleeve she set Lucca to her breast. She felt bad for misjudging Cohen. Clearly his feelings were hurt when she called him a thief, and her accusation he would steal Lucca from her only rubbed salt in the wound. The reality of the situation was she had to trust this man she hardly knew with her life and her son's. *His son's.*

Cohen entered the room with a large covered tray. He balanced it precariously as he shut the door, giving her a roguish grin. "I raided the galley, my lady."

She could not help but smile back at him as he crossed the room and set the tray on the table. "Do you not have a cook?"

He took the lid off the tray and poured a cup of steaming brown liquid. "I do, however he is staying somewhere in town. I do not require most of the crew to stay aboard during the winter months. You will become bored with my simple fare before long, so I hope for both of our sakes you can cook."

When she nodded he smiled, crossing the room to hand her the cup. Cassie took a sip of the hot coffee and sputtered. It tasted bitter, burnt, and horrible.

He gave her a remorseful look. "Is it that bad?"

She giggled and nodded.

He shrugged. "See? I told you I was not much of a cook."

"I prefer chocolate in the morning anyway," Cassie reassured him.

Taking a drink from his own cup he made a face. "It is pretty bad." He chuckled, setting the cup down. "Well, I suppose after my meager breakfast offering is choked down I shall take you on a tour of the galley. You can decide for yourself what supplies are needed and I will have them purchased right away so we do not starve before the ice flows melt."

Cassie smiled and looked down at the plate of blackened toast he offered her. "Perhaps we should tour the galley now." She laughed at his sheepish expression.

With a flick of his wrist he flipped the toast into the brazier and set the plate back on the table. "Perhaps you are right."

When Cassie finished feeding Lucca, Cohen took the baby and burped him. Then he offered her his free arm. "Come on, the galley is this way."

They walked down the corridor in the opposite direction from the exit. At the end of the passageway he led her down a short flight of stairs and into an enormous kitchen.

"Oh my!" Cassie giggled. "I had no idea a ship's galley was so big!"

Cohen shot her an amused look. "It takes a crew of twenty-five to sail this ship so it has to be big in order to prepare three full meals each day and seat everyone."

Cassie glanced at him and frowned.

"What?"

"Nothing, really, I was just wondering why you took a ship to Bath instead of a coach, when sailing makes you seasick."

Cohen grinned mischievously. "I booked passage on the ship to see you again, of course."

She looked away, both embarrassed and pleased at his candid admission.

"From the moment I saw you I was smitten."

The baby fussed, and Cassie returned her gaze to him.

He lowered the baby from his shoulder, cradling him in his arms. "Yes, I did," he crooned, "Your mother was so beautiful in that pretty pink dress I could not resist kissing her." He smiled when the baby cooed and sucked his fist.

Cassie blushed, remembering his kisses in the dark room. A small shiver of excitement slid down her spine. He noticed her dress, felt desire for her when her husband did not. He was young, handsome, funny, and patient, where the earl was old, crippled, sour, and uninterested. *Why could I not have married the man who makes my heart beat with exhilaration, rather than the one who makes it slow with defeat and repudiation?*

"Cassie?"

She blinked, refocusing her gaze. Cohen regarded her with knowing green orbs, the same ones gracing the face of their son. Forcing the thoughts from her mind she blinked again. "Yes?"

He tipped his chin toward the far wall. "The supplies are kept in the cupboards over there."

"Yes, of course." Cassie ducked her head and hurried to inspect the cupboards.

Twenty minutes later she sent Cohen on his way, armed with a list of obtainable items. She took Lucca back to the master cabin and settled into a chair by the brazier where she gazed at the sleeping baby, trying to put her feelings and emotions to rights. *Perhaps my loneliness makes me gravitate to the comté. Maybe I am suffering from some kind of post pregnancy melancholy. Am I only attracted to him because I failed to gain my husband's approval? He is so gentle and commanding with me and Lucca...* She gasped. *Could I be falling in love with him?*

The baby's lips pursed for a second, the corner of his cupid bows twitching. What did the future hold for her and Lucca?

Loud male voices carried from the upper deck. Cassie set Lucca carefully in his basket and moved to the door. She opened it a crack and peered out into the corridor. The guard was gone. The voices carried clearly down the passageway.

"Where is Ashton?" The voice carried a strange foreign burr she could not place.

Someone replied in French.

"Ashton, ye scoundrel, where the devil are ye?"

Cassie froze. *Did the earl's men find us already? What am I going to do? Will Rennie and his men keep my presence hidden?*

Footsteps sounded on the stairs. "Ashton? Damn it! Ye would think ye could hire someone on this floatin' monstrosity who speaks English!"

Panicked, Cassie ducked back into the room. She did not have the key to lock the door from the inside. She snatched up Lucca and darted into the bedchamber. After closing the door, she leaned against it, and held her breath. The silence was broken by the parlor door banging against the wall.

"Ashton?"

Footsteps crossed to the door. *Please do not let him try the knob.* The steps paused; then continued on. After a moment she heard the top of the brandy decanter clink back into place. A soft squish confirmed her suspicions the man had settled on the settee and intended to stay for a while. If Cohen did not get back soon the baby would wake to be fed, and the man in the other room would surely hear. Cassie eased from the door and tiptoed to the bed. She cringed when the frame squeaked as she perched on the edge of the mattress. *Oh God! What if he heard the noise?* When he did not come to investigate she set Lucca's basket on the bed beside her.

The silence stretched as taunt as her nerves. Her back began to ache from the strain of sitting so still, afraid to move lest she betray her presence. Finally, when she thought she would faint from the sheer terror of the unknown, she became aware of Cohen's commanding baritone up on deck. Footfalls clattered down the stairs and the door to the parlor opened.

"Forton, you old devil! How are you?"

Cassie let out an audible sigh at Cohen's friendly banter.

"Fine, just fine, Ashton." The sound of them slapping each other on the back carried through the door.

"What are you doing here?"

"I finished a dig in Scotland and decided to spend a month or two in Bath. I'm heading for Sicily as soon as the ice melts. Anyway, my ship suffered some major damage on the last trip, and I was hoping to commission another here in Bristol or Portsmouth when I saw the *Discovery* docked in the bay. What brings ye here, Ashton?"

"The usual." Cohen chuckled. "I, too, am waiting for the ice to break so I might head for home."

"I see. I would have thought ye would have left before the ice?"

"I would have, but Everton was up to his usual tricks. I stayed around to pilfer a few treasures from his greedy hands. Speaking of treasures, have you met Cassandra?"

Cassie noted the surprise in Forton's reply. "Cassandra? I've met no lady here."

Footsteps crossed to the door and Cassie stood as it opened.

Cohen looked puzzled for a moment before realisation dawned on his face. "Cassie, were you hiding in here?"

She stepped away from the bed. "I did not know if he was one of the earl's men or not."

"I am sorry Forton frightened you. He tends to frighten most young maidens." His eyes twinkled with humor as Forton protested goodnaturedly from beyond the door.

"Hey, I donna' frighten all the maidens. After all, I did find one who was not cowed by my size."

Cassie understood his jest when Cohen led her from the room. A large red haired man stood in the centre of the parlor. He was taller than Cohen by almost a full foot. His broad shoulders and large meaty arms were enough make even the sturdiest maiden give him careful consideration. His rotund belly bulged casually over a brass belt buckle as large as Cassie's hand, almost level with her eyes. Thick legs braced in larger than average boots completed the picture of a powerfully built man. He smiled, his droopy red moustache twitching as his eyes glowed with merriment.

"Cassie, this is Augustus Forton, my good friend and fellow artifact hunter. Forton, this is Lady Cassandra Everton." Cohen squeezed her hand.

Forton's eyes widened. "By the Saints that be! Are ye saying this lovely lass is Everton's latest wife?"

Cohen nodded with a cheeky grin. "That she is."

The big man gave her a wide smile. "Well, then, it is pleased I be to meet ye, my lady." He gave her an elegant bow for someone so large.

"Thank you, Mister Forton." Cassie smiled shyly.

"See, you do so frighten the ladies." Cohen chuckled, giving Cassie a wink. "Do not worry, he may be big but like most Scotsmen his appearance is the only thing scary about him."

Forton tipped his head back, his booming guffaws reverberating off the walls. When he regained his composure he smiled sheepishly. "Ach, 'tis true, my lady. A fox has more bite than I."

Cohen showed Cassie to the settee, settling in the chair beside it as Forton lowered his bulk into the other chair. The Scotsman studied at her with a curious look. "How is it ye have come to be on Ashton's ship, Lady Everton?"

"Please, call me Cassie. Cohen stole me from my husband's house two nights ago."

The look on Forton's face said it all. His expression went from incredulous to gleeful within a span of a few brief seconds. "Ye scoundrel, not enough thrills so ye decide to steal the lecher's wife, too?"

Cohen grinned. "In my defence Forton, I had to rescue my son."

Forton looked even more surprised. "Ye have a son?"

As if on cue, Lucca began to wail from the bedchamber. Cohen stayed Cassie with a hand on her shoulder as she started to get up. "I will get him."

She nodded as he rose and crossed to the door.

He disappeared inside for a moment and reappeared with Lucca tucked securely in the crook of his arm. He stopped in front of the

Scotsman. "May I present my son, Lucca."

Forton took the small bundle in his large hands and rocked the baby with a gentleness any mother would envy. "Ach, look at the wee laddie, the image of his sire, I'd say. There be no doubt he is yers Ashton, for the eyes do not deceive, eh?"

"I thought the same the first time I looked upon him." He took the baby when he began to fuss and handed him to Cassie. "I will tell you the whole story whilst Cassie feeds him in the other room. I will send one of Rennie's men to the inn to bring back some afternoon tea."

The Scotsman stood as she rose to her feet. "Until later, Lady Cassie," he said with a slight bow.

Cassie hurried to the bedchamber to attend to Lucca's needs in private.

Chapter Fifteen

Forton pushed back his chair and dropped his napkin on the table. A sailor, serving as a footman for dinner, refilled his wineglass without having been asked. The Scotsman lifted the glass and regarded Cassie and Cohen over the rim. "So, tell me, Ashton, what are yer plans?"

Cohen pushed back his own chair and stood. He crossed to the fire and sat in one of the chairs. "As soon as the ice breaks up I will be sailing to France. I am taking Cassie and Lucca home to meet my family."

"Surely ye have realized Everton will eventually find ye and come for his wife, what then?" Forton followed and sat in the chair opposite him.

Cassie sat on the settee. Forton asked the question she wondered about herself, and she was keen to hear Cohen's solution.

"I was thinking about taking Cassie and Lucca on the proposed dig in Spain."

"How long do ye think ye can run before Everton corners ye?" Forton shook his head.

"A year is long enough for Everton to give up and have her legally declared dead."

She felt herself blanch at the admission. *Declared dead? Then what?*

Forton leaned forward. "Come now, ye and I both know Everton isna going to give up something of his without a fight. If it takes the rest of his life he will hunt ye down."

For the first time, Cassie saw Cohen look defeated. He hung his head. "He will have to kill me before I let him have my son, and I will never let him take Cassie from her child."

It was hopeless. Cassie felt her heart pinch painfully. The earl would find them and there was no doubt Cohen would give his life to keep Lucca and her from him.

Forton settled back in his chair and pondered his friend with a tight-lipped expression. "Then we best come up with a plan, eh?"

Cohen shook his head. "I do not want to get you involved. It was my folly that got us into this mess."

"Folly is putting it mildly, my friend, but donna count me out. I, too, have a score to settle with that whore-son Everton. Makes no matter to me who reckons with him or how it is done as long as he is put in his place, preferably in his grave."

At Cassie's gasp, both men looked at her.

"Perhaps you should explain to Cassie just what kind of monster Everton is," Cohen said with a hard look in his eye.

Forton clenched his jaw. "The bastard blew up a dig, killin' my father, sister, and a dozen workers. He doesn't care who he hurts, long as he gets the prize. His last wife was the cousin of a mutual friend. He tormented the woman with her supposed inability to get with child until she finally killed herself, when it is he who is unable to sire a child, ye see."

Cassie put the back of her hand to her mouth. The man whose love she sought to gain all those months was, in truth, a monster. Did her father have any idea who he pledged her hand to? No, she refused to believe her father would have sentenced her to a life of misery if he knew of the earl's baser qualities.

Cohen leaned back in his chair, his gaze locked on the coals flickering in the brazier. "So, what do you think we should do?"

The baby awoke in the bedchamber and whimpered.

Cassie got up and hurried to him.

"We find a way to stop the bastard." Cassie heard Forton say as she closed the door. A shiver ran down her spine. *Blood is going to be shed because of my sinful action. God will surely condemn me to an eternity in hell now.*

She was just finished changing Lucca when Cohen poked his head around the door.

"Cassie, Forton and I have a few errands to run. Is there anything you need me to get for you?"

"I am almost out of swaddling for Lucca."

Cohen nodded.

"Shall I make dinner for us tonight?"

He smiled. "Would it be too terribly inconvenient if Forton were to stay the night?"

She shrugged. "If he does not mind simple fare it would not be a problem. Did you get all the supplies on the list?"

"They were delivered a few minutes ago. I had Alexander, one of Rennie's men, put them in the galley."

Cassie nodded and set Lucca back in his basket.

"If you are worried about being left here alone, I will stay."

"I will be fine. It was silly of me to be afraid before." Cassie smiled her thanks.

He crossed the room and took her hand in his. "No, it was not. I promise you Rennie and his men will do everything in their power to protect you. You are safe here, Everton has no power over this ship or my crew as they belong to France."

Cassie smiled at him doubtfully. "I thought the Emperor gave you this ship?"

"He did, but in the end I serve the Emperor. The artifacts I steal from Everton, and those like him, I turn over to the Emperor at his command."

She stared at him wide eyed. "Do you mean to say you steal for the Emperor?"

He shrugged. "I guess you could say that. It is my job to keep an eye on Everton. Anything he takes from another country through ill means I steal back. The Emperor returns the artifacts to their country of origin, for a price of course. In the end they get their artifacts back, and France gets an ally."

She furrowed her brow, wondering why France needed an ally. Before she could voice her thoughts, Cohen placed a kiss on the palm of her hand. A familiar tingle started where his lips touched; then traveled up her arm, making her head spin. He straightened and was out the door before she came to her senses. She picked up Lucca's basket and headed for the galley. When she arrived at the kitchen she found Alexander there, unpacking crates of provisions.

"*Mademoiselle, les sacs d'epicerie sont ici. Magnifique, oui?*" He smiled at her.

Cassie smiled back and set Lucca's basket down on the large

dining table. "Wonderful. I do not suppose you understand English?"

He laughed, displaying a dazzling set of straight white teeth. "*Oui, Mademoiselle*. I speak, ah, some English, *oui.*"

"Good. Perhaps you can teach me some French, and I will help you with your English." With a giggle, she picked up a loaf of fresh bread and held it up. "Bread."

He nodded. "*Oui, pain*." He smiled. "Bread."

She grinned. "*Pain*." She held up the next items. "Eggs, cheese, and potatoes."

He nodded again, his eyes twinkling. "*Oeufs, fromage, pomme de terre*. Ah, eggz, cheez, potatoz," he repeated with a triumphant grin.

"Yes. *Oui!*" She smiled.

They spent the afternoon teaching each other and cooking. For the first time since her marriage to the earl, Cassie found herself relaxing and enjoying herself. Before long the galley was put to rights and the evening meal made.

Cassie looked up at Cohen's laugh. He leaned on the door frame, his eyes dancing with mirth. She lifted an enquiring eyebrow. "What?"

"You have a little flour there." He pointed.

She brushed her cheek.

The corner of his mouth curled up. "You missed it." He straightened and crossed to where she stood. When she looked up he gently wiped the offending smear away.

Swallowing, she steeled herself as his fingers stroked the skin along her jaw. Her hands began to tremble so badly she wrapped them together in her apron to keep him from seeing.

His eyes darkened; then his gaze shifted to her lips. "I think you missed some here, too," he murmured, just before he dipped his head and touched his lips to hers.

Her heart flip-flopped as his lips caressed hers in a sweet symphony of sensation. She melted into him with a sigh. Then his lips were no longer there. She opened her eyes and blinked up at him in dazed confusion as he stepped back.

His eyes smoldered with passion and humor. He looked over her head. "*Bonjour,* Alex."

Cassie wiped her hands on her apron and busied herself setting the table. What would the sailor think of her wanton behavior? She listened to the two men converse in French, the elegant words rolling off their tongues like a wren's lilting song.

"Ah, there ye are."

Cassie looked up as the Scotsman strolled across the floor.

"I hope ye donna' mind me staying for dinner, lass."

"It is no problem, Mr. Forton. I would be glad of the company." She smiled, genuinely pleased he was staying.

He gave her a humble grin, pulled out a chair, and lowered his considerable bulk into it. "Please lass, call me Auggie. I was Auggie long before I was a mister."

Cassie could not help but like the man. "Then you must call me, Cassie."

She turned away from the table and stopped short as Cohen stepped in front of her. He smiled and twirled his finger around in a circle. She lifted a brow, puzzled, until he turned her around to untie the apron at her waist.

"Sit." He tossed the apron on top of the counter. "Alex can serve the meal."

She slid into the chair he pulled out for her. He was always a gentleman.

Alex served the hearty chicken stew and fresh baked biscuits. Both men dug in with relish.

"I am sorry it is not the fanciest of fares, I am used to preparing aught but simple meals." Cassie picked up her spoon.

Cohen looked up from his second spoonful. "It is a fine meal, Cassie. If you are not careful I may have to fire my own cook."

The Scotsman nodded in agreement, polishing off his first biscuit, and reaching for a second. "Aye lass, a fine meal ye have prepared for sure."

Cassie smiled, assured their compliments were sincere and turned her attention to her own food.

"Auggie and I have been talking."

She paused, the spoon part way to her lips and regarded Cohen expectantly.

He smiled. "We thought it would be best if we passed you off as my wife for the time being. You would be safer aboard the ship if the men believe you are married to me. It would preserve your reputation as well. We have to decide what to do. We spotted a couple of Pinkerton's in town today. This means Everton has already figured out we are here. We have to move, either by carriage or we can chance the sea. The weather has been warming, and I think, if we hug the shore, most of the ice flow should be melted by the time we reach the channel. It will be dangerous this early in the year, but I believe it is our best chance."

Her mind froze, and she dropped the spoon to the table with a clatter. *My husband has found us. Will he kill us as Cohen fears?*

"Cassie?"

She blinked, pushing her thoughts back into the tumultuous recesses of her mind. Her eyes focused on Cohen. "I am sorry. You were saying?"

He leaned forward and gripped her hand in his. "I want to know what you want to do. I think we should sail. It would be more comfortable for you and Lucca, but it is your choice."

She stared at his hand for a moment, warm, solid, and secure. *Is he really asking me? No one ever asked me what I wanted before. Perhaps if my parents asked me if I wanted to marry the earl, none of this would have ever happened.* For the first time in her life she felt the thrill of making her own decision. She looked up. "I think we should sail."

Cohen nodded grimly. "All right. I will have Rennie round up the men tonight, and we will weigh anchor at first tide." Lucca began to fuss in his basket by the door. "Go and look after our son. I will have Alex clean up here. You must be tired from putting the galley to rights. Take my bed, and do not wait up, Forton and I have things to do to ready for the journey."

Cassie nodded, scooping up the baby, and heading for the cabin.

Chapter Sixteen

Cassie stood on the deck, clutching her cloak as the wind slapped the edges against her skirts. The English coastline slid by in muted tones of brown and grey. She could just make out a group of bulls huddled under a large oak.

"Cassie?

She turned around.

Cohen strolled toward her with a weary smile. His breath puffed from his mouth in small white clouds. "What are you doing up here in the cold?" His eyes raked her from head to toe. "You must be freezing."

"I was bored. Your cook chased me from the galley with a broom." She crossed her arms across her chest and added crossly, "I only wanted to help."

His eyes twinkled. "I am afraid Perrier is very particular about who is allowed in his domain. If you like, I will speak to him."

She shook her head. "I would not want to make him angry with me."

He smiled. "You are right; he might take his spite out on our dinner." He consulted his fob watch then looked up. Ominous black clouds rolled across the sky, lightning turning the far horizon phosphorescent. "I fear we are in for a rough night."

The words barely left his lips than the sky rumbled and unleashed its fury, the rain pelting them with vigor. Within seconds the deluge turned to hail the size of walnuts. Cassie let out a squeal as Cohen grasped her hand and pulled her below to the cabin.

Laughing, she jerked off her cloak and tossed it across the back of a chair as they entered the parlor. She looked at Cohen. His hair was plastered against his head, water dripping down his face onto his sodden coat. *Even half drowned, he is handsome.* She looked away and crossed to the fire, shaking her hair loose from its tidy bun to dry. Cohen joined her and offered a towel.

"Thank you."

He smiled, draping his own over his head and rubbing it zealously. "You will need to batten down the hatches."

"What does that mean?" She wiped her face.

He finished drying his hair and slung the damp cloth around his neck. "It means, make sure everything that is not secured to the wall or the floor is stored away in those big trunks over there." As if to emphasize his words, the ship lurched to the side. Cassie lost her balance and staggered into Cohen. He wrapped his arms around her with a grin. "So they do not roll around," he finished with a cheeky grin.

"Oh." Her breath caught in her throat as she gazed at him, his arms tightening and his look heated. His gaze shifted to her mouth and without thinking she slipped her tongue between her lips to moisten them. *Is he going to kiss me? I certainly hope so.* His head moved leisurely toward hers, his eyes darkening. *I should not let him kiss me. I am still married to the earl.* When his lips touched hers something akin to liquid fire shot through her limbs. Her body trembled, her knees turning to rubber as she sagged against him. Before she knew it she was in his embrace as he carried her to the bedchamber. She moaned against his lips when he laid her on the bed and lowered himself beside her. When his lips left hers to travel down the sensitive column of her neck she stiffened. *What am I doing?* "Please, we cannot, I cannot..."

"Yes, we can," the words were murmured against her neck. His lips traced their way downward, leaving tingles of sensation in their wake until they came to the neckline of her modest blouse. He kissed the sensitive skin along her collarbone as his fingers deftly undid the laces.

I should protest. I should stop him. However, when she took a deep breath, no words came out, only a sigh of pleasure as his lips warmed her breast.

His mouth played there for a moment before he moaned and sat up, his eyes dark and restless. "If I do not stop now, I will not be able to. It is too soon since Lucca's birth for me to want you this way."

The euphoric feelings vanished as the reality of what she was doing came crashing down on her. *I am immoral and wanton. I will surely be cast into the fiery pits of hell for all eternity. No other woman could be as thoroughly impure. I am supposed to be a good minister's daughter.* She choked back a sob, tears streaming down her face.

"Cassie?" His brows furrowed. "Cassie, what is it?"

She squeezed her eyes shut to block out his concern. "I am a sinful person."

"Why would you say such a thing?"

"I-you-every time you touch me... I feel all these things I should not."

He chuckled. "There is nothing wrong with enjoying being made love to, Cassie."

She opened her eyes and glared at him. "Yes, there is. I should not feel these things. My husband...."

The smile vanished from his face though his eyes still twinkled with mirth. "Your husband, what?"

She looked down at her hands. "My husband did not make me feel the way you do. It is evil of me to be so...wanton."

This time Cohen threw back his head and laughed. She scurried from the bed and turned her back on him. Clenching her teeth, she jerked the front of her blouse together and tightened the laces. *How dare he make fun of me!*

His laughter receded into chuckles of amusement. "Cassie."

She ignored him, seething with anger barely kept in check.

"Cassie." His voice sobered. The bed creaked before his hand caught her fingers as she knotted the strings.

"Leave me be." She batted it away.

"I did not mean to laugh. I am sorry," he said softly.

Cassie lifted her chin to glower at him. "You were making light of my feelings."

He gave her a pleading look. "I know, and for that I am sorry." He pulled her toward him. "Cass, you are not wanton. Every woman has the right to feel passion and desire. It is not wrong to enjoy it when I make love to you."

Her face flamed with embarrassment. "It *is* wrong, do you not see? You are not my husband."

Cohen tilted her head up to look her in the eye. "Lord Everton is the one who is wrong. It was wrong of him to marry you and not take care to see to your satisfaction before his own. Just as it was wrong of him to treat you like a child instead of the beautiful and desirable woman you are. It is not sinful to enjoy making love when two people love each other."

Her breath caught in her throat. *Did he just say he loves me?* She looked deep into his eyes, searching for the truth she wanted so desperately to believe. It was there. She saw the love shining in his eyes. *He does love me.*

The baby began to fuss in his basket by the bed. Cohen stepped away from her and picked Lucca up with a grimace; then gave her a lopsided grin. "I think our son needs a change." He handed her the baby, pressing a soft kiss on her lips. "See to our son while I go speak with Rennie and the crew."

* * * *

Boom!

Cassie looked up from settling Lucca, freshly swaddled and fed in his basket. The ship shuddered and listed to one side. Screams rent the air and fear clawed at her insides. What was happening? Was the storm tearing apart the ship? She snatched up Lucca's basket and folded a blanket over the top to keep out the wind. Tucking it under her arm she hurried out the cabin door and up top to see what was happening.

Smoke filled the air, its thick burning stench making her cough. Covering her mouth and nose with the edge of her cloak she made her way across the deck, straining to see. A large gap in the railing appeared as the smoke shifted, flames licking at the charred and splintered remains. She spotted Cohen standing by the gap, shouting and waving his arms. Slipping and sliding across the rolling deck, she scrambled toward him.

Cohen turned, spying her. "Cassie! Go back below!"

A large wave crashed over the deck, splattering her skirts, and pulling her off balance. She tumbled forward and Cohen grasped her arm to steady her. She caught her breath as he took the basket from her and tucked it securely under his free arm.

The thunderous noise of the storm almost drowned out her voice. "What is going on?"

"There is a ship firing its cannons on us, probably Everton's."

Before Cassie could question him further there was a brilliant flash of light from the bow. Timber screeched as it shattered into thousands of splinters and rained down upon them. Cassie flailed helplessly, falling onto the planking. The ship trembled and rolled as she fought to regain her footing on the slippery surface. Rolling onto her knees she lifted her head and looked around. Cohen was gone.

Terrified, she scanned the vessel but he and the baby were nowhere to be seen. "Cohen! Cohen!"

A burly shape manifested out of the smoke and gloom. "Cassie, lass!"

She squinted as the shape took on the form of the Scotsman. "Auggie? Cohen was here... I do not see him now... He is gone... Lucca, too!"

Forton grasped her arm, hauling her to her feet. "Come on, lassie! We need to get to the row boat. The *Discovery*, she's sinkin' fast."

Cassie shook her head, terror rooting her to the spot. "No! I cannot leave without Lucca!"

The giant of a man lifted her up and slung her over his shoulder. "I'm sure the wee bairn is safe with Cohen." He trotted across to the other side of the ship. When they reached the railing he set her down; then swung up and over it. "Climb down after me, lassie, so I kin steady ye." He disappeared over the side.

A blast shook the ship and the wooden planks dropped out from under her. Cassie frantically grasped for anything to keep from falling. Screaming, she desperately tried to slow her descent into the unknown. Pain on the side of her head registered briefly before her fall was stopped short by an icy stab as it knocked the wind from her lungs. Freezing water rushed over her head, distorting all the sounds around her. Panic took hold of her sluggish mind. Kicking and clawing, she fought her waterlogged skirts and cloak to get to the surface, her lungs burning with the need for air as her mind began to fade. *I am going to die. I never even had the chance to tell Cohen I love him.*

Something grabbed her arm, and she opened her mouth to protest without thinking. Icy water filled her lungs. Blackness threatened to take her as her sluggish mind slowed. Without warning, her head popped free of the water, and she spewed up salty seawater; then inhaled a huge gulp of air. Coughing and sputtering, she was hauled over the side of a small row boat. She lay there, limp, unable to move, gasping for breath. Shadows blurred and moved before her eyes.

"Cassie...lass...off...wet clothes...Cassie?"

She rolled herself into a small ball and lay shivering uncontrollably, unable to make sense of the voices and shadows around her. Hands removed her clothes, but she could not will her numb mind and body to respond. Something dry was wrapped around her before she was lifted and set down again, her teeth chattering.

"Cassie. Kin ye hear me lass?"

Cassie turned her head. Her fuzzy vision registered the large form of Forton. "Auggie?" He smiled; at least, she thought he did.

"Aye, lassie. Ye got a bad bump on yer noggin' ye did."

She put a hand to her throbbing head and felt the lump forming there. When she moved her hand, her fingers were sticky and wet. She stared uncomprehendingly at the red smear on her fingers as nausea overwhelmed her. Dizzy and disoriented, she tried to focus her eyes, but the voices faded away.

* * * *

Gravel scraped the bottom of the boat. Cassie forced her eyes open. It was dark. Something flapped above her... The distinct sound of rain splattering on a tarp... Something crinkled and drops of cold rain hit her face.

"Cassie, lass, ye need to get up."

Hands helped her to her feet. She swayed on wobbly legs and leaned against a hard chest. Powerful arms swept her up and cradled her against warmth. "Cohen?"

"Nay, lass. It is jus' me, Auggie."

Cassie felt each footstep in her head as he carried her. She moaned. In her mind Cohen stood, holding the basket. Then he was gone in a puff of black smoke and soot. "Where is Lucca?" She felt rather than heard the catch in Auggie's breath.

"They're both gone, lass."

She tried to lift her head but the effort was too much. "Gone?" Her aching brain could not make the connection. *Gone?*

"Rest now, lassie, I promised Ashton I would take care of ye if anything happened to him. Yer safe with me."

Gone? Something happened. Gone where? The words circled around in her mind again and again without her being able to piece them together.

Chapter Seventeen

Cassie stared at the pale green canvas stretched above her head. She shivered, wrapping Auggie's tartan cloak tighter around herself. *Cohen and Lucca are gone, killed by my husband's men, down into the depths of the unforgiving sea with the ship.* Her heart and mind, dull with grief, spoke the words, but her tears were spent. *What do I do now? Where will I go? Will the earl think I, too, am dead? If he finds out I am alive, will he seek to have me returned to him?*

"Cassie, lass."

She turned her head as Auggie pulled back the flap on the makeshift tent.

He looked past her, not meeting her eye. "I brought back a coach and something to eat."

Cassie turned her face away and looked back at the tent roof.

He continued in the same odd flat tone he used to tell her of their deaths. "I commissioned a ship. I thought maybe ye could come back with me to Marseilles. I need to tell Ashton's family of ..." His voice caught with sorrow. "I need to tell them he is...dead."

Cassie stared at a bead of condensation trickling slowly down the underside of the canvas. *Go to France, where Cohen's brother and sisters lived, with all their children.*

"Cassie?"

She nodded, unable to force the words past her swollen, salt cracked lips.

It was silent for a moment. She ignored him, continuing to watch blindly the bead of water sliding until it crossed the seam. It trickled down the wall, fading from her line of vision.

"I brought ye some clothes. I thought yers might be crusty with salt and as uncomfortable as mine."

She caught the flash of his coat out of the corner of her eye. The paper package crinkled as he placed it by her head. The tent flap lifted, momentarily brightening the interior before rustling back into place. *I am alone.* She let her breath escape in a crisp whoosh of cool white air, and then rolled onto her side and sat up. Her head swam, her vision blurring at the sudden movement. Once she became accustomed to being upright she reached for the package. Slipping off the string holding the paper she unrolled it. Nestled inside was a chemise, a soft blue wool skirt, a simple white blouse and a darker blue cloak. It was nice of Auggie to think of her comfort and purchase the garments. She must remember to thank him for his care these last two days.

She got dressed slowly, shivering in the frigid spring air. It did not matter if she froze to death. *Nothing really matters anymore.* She stood up carefully so as not to jar her still tender head and wandered from the tent. A coach sat opposite the fire. Two brown horses, each standing with a hind foot cocked in rest, dozed in their harness while the coachman waited.

Auggie looked up from his seat on a stump. He gave her a weak smile which she did not bother to return and held her hands out to the fire, staring into the dying flames. *Soon the flames will disappear completely and leave me to face the cold world alone...again.*

"Cassie?"

She did not look up. A tin trencher of food entered her line of vision.

"Ye must eat something, lass."

She reached out a shaky hand and took the crude trencher even though she did not want to. It was easier to humor Auggie than listen to him nag. She glanced at the contents. The thick slice of bread, roasted chicken breast, and still steaming potato did nothing to tempt her appetite. Heaving a dejected groan, she lowered herself to the damp grass and picked at the meal. Once she picked apart the food and pushed it around for a sufficient amount of time she set the trencher beside her. She watched as Auggie kicked dirt on the remains of the campfire. *Gone, like Cohen and Lucca. Gone, like my will to go on by myself.*

Auggie crossed to where she sat and held out his hand. Cassie was aware of the heat as he sealed her cold fingers in his and pulled her up. She allowed him to lead her to the coach and help her in.

Once he was seated, he tapped on the roof, and they headed for the docks of the tiny town of Penzance. *We were lucky, he told me... Was that yesterday, perhaps?* The days and nights ran into themselves in an undistinguishable blur of heartache. *Yes, perhaps yesterday he told me the storm and the sea current washed us ashore only a few short miles from the seaside town. Lucky, why do I not feel so lucky? I do not feel anything.*

She turned and stared out the window unseeingly as the tears she thought were dried and gone wet her eyelids and trickled down her cheeks. *Why did I not die?* Anger pricked her chest, the first vibrant emotion she acknowledged since her near drowning. *Auggie is why I did not die. Damn him! It is his fault I am trapped in this cocoon of pain. Damn him.* She bit her lip. *No, that is not fair. It is not his fault. There is only one man I should hate. Lord Everton.*

The damp forest gave way to the cobbled streets of the town. Cheery looking people bustled here and there, on their way to something or someone important. She swiped the tears from her face angrily and crossed her arms. Crying would not bring Lucca back. It was a sign of weakness, something only pathetic women did according to the earl.

The coach pulled up in front of the little dock where two small merchant ships and a large schooner were moored. Auggie hoped out and turned to help her. She climbed down and shuffled across the dock with him, oblivious to where they were going. She looked down at her feet as they made their way up the gangplank, not bothering to look up when the captain of the ship greeted them.

"Welcome, Mister Forton, Comtésse Ashton."

Cassie blinked. Comtésse *Ashton?*

Auggie squeezed her hand. "Thank ye, Captain Smith. I appreciate ye taking us on board at such short notice."

"It was the least I could do for you and Ashton's widow."

This time Cassie's head snapped up of its own accord. She stared at the captain; then Auggie. Before she could question either man, Auggie tucked her hand in the crook of his arm and towed her forward down the deck.

"I will see Comtésse Ashton is settled in her cabin and be back to discuss payment."

The captain nodded.

Cassie followed Auggie down the corridor to a set of doors. "Why did you call me Comtésse Ashton?"

He glanced down at her as he opened the door. "Under the circumstances I thought it best to let everyone think ye are Cohen's widow going home to see his family. Everton will be looking for ye, and it is more acceptable to travel un-chaperoned in the guise of a widow."

Cassie entered the room. It was sparsely furnished but comfortable looking. Two chairs flanked the modest brazier; a small bed took up one corner with a large sea trunk placed at the foot of it. A square table with four chairs took up the other corner.

Auggie released her hand. "I've taken the liberty of arranging fer a local lass to act as yer maid and to accompany ye to the shops before we leave. Purchase anything ye might need on Cohen's account."

Cassie nodded, her heart pinching with sorrow at the mention of Cohen's name. She sat in one of the chairs and stared into the fire. A moment later she heard the door close behind Auggie. She did not feel like shopping. She was so tired. If only she could fall asleep and wake up to find all that happened to her was just a bad dream. To wake up in the old bed she shared with her sister, Beth.

A knock on the door roused her from her thoughts. She looked to the door without enthusiasm. "Come in."

It swung open and Alex stood on the threshold with his hat in his hands. "*Bonjour*, Lady...Everton."

Cassie rose from her chair and crossed the room, stopping in front of the sailor. "Alex. Is it truly you?"

"*Oui, Mademoiselle*. I 'ave a...." He paused for a moment, floundering for the words in English. "I 'ave taken position on ze ship —I sail home."

Cassie reached out and clutched his hand, turning her eyes to his in a pleading gesture. "Please, Alex, tell me Cohen and Lucca are alive. Tell me you saw them after the blast."

The young sailor dropped his gaze to the floor. "I am sorry. Comté Ashton...gone, *Mademoiselle*." He gently pried her fingers from his, and then reached into the satchel at his feet. He pulled out the oriental box Cohen gave Cassie on the trip to Bath and handed it to her. "I found 'zis. I thought you would…want, *oui*?"

Cassie nodded slowly and took the box from his hand. The cool wooden surface was warped but still glossy. Without thinking, she opened the lid. The hinges creaked, stiff from the salt water. Inside, nestled in the faded, crusty velvet interior was the little jade elephant. "Thank you," she whispered, struggling to keep the tears that welled up in her eyes in check.

He nodded and turned to leave; then paused, looking back at her. "You need any zing; you come to me, *oui*?"

Cassie nodded, and then he was gone.

A young girl peered into the room. "My lady? Mister Forton, sent for me."

She placed the box on the table.

The young girl gave her braid a tug and worried her bottom lip for a moment before she spoke again. "Mister Forton said to take you shopping."

Cassie nodded again and headed out the door. Men scurried back and forth on the deck, loading supplies. She looked around but did not see Auggie anywhere. Lifting her skirts clear of the disarray of cargo, she made her way down the gangplank, the new maid trailing in her wake.

A sign on the second shop caught her eye. She paused; then opened the door. A young clerk looked up from his paper cluttered desk. "Can I help you?"

"Is this Mr. Penning's office?"

The clerk smiled. "Yes, it is. Do you have an appointment with him, Miss…?"

"Lady Everton," Cassie supplied. "No, but I would like to speak with him about a most pressing matter if he is in."

The clerk nodded and stood. He gestured to a chair against the wall. "If you would be so kind as to wait a moment, I will inform him you are here." When she nodded he hurried through a door in the far wall. After a moment an older man followed him into the room. His grey moustache twitched as he smiled at her and pushed his spectacles further up his nose. "What can I do for you, Lady Everton?"

Taking a deep breath she looked him straight in the eye. "I would like to petition for a divorce."

The man did not even blink. "All right, if you will kindly follow me to my office, Lady Everton." He swept his hand to the side to indicate she should precede him.

She motioned for the maid to wait; then walked ahead of the man into his office. He waited until she was settled in a straight-backed chair in front of his desk and closed the door. After he had taken his seat opposite her he leaned his elbows on the desk top and smiled.

"Now, Lady Everton, why not start at the beginning and explain to me why you want to legally vacate your husband's control."

Cassie explained the situation, her face flushing when she briefly mentioned Cohen's midnight visit.

Mr. Penning listened intently, showing no sign of judgment at her tale. When she was done he leaned back in his chair and contemplated her for a moment before he spoke. "As I am sure you are aware, Lady Everton, a divorce is both a costly procedure and a social stigma." When Cassie nodded he continued. "I believe you might have a case for an annulment of your marriage, however. The fact you have not been married the full three years required by parliament might be your only problem. You say, Lord Everton, had already commissioned a place for you at St. Catherine's Convent?"

"Yes, the night I ran away."

"If Lord Everton did, in fact, make this arrangement, then is it not also likely he is willing to arrange for an annulment?"

She lowered her gaze to her hands clutched in her lap. "The fact that my son is now dead might change his mind. He wants an heir desperately before he dies, you see, and I am the means to that end, or so he thinks. It is obvious to all he is incapable of fathering a child." She stopped, her face burning with embarrassment.

"I see." The room was silent. Finally when she was about to get up and apologise for wasting his time, his chair creaked.

He cleared his throat. "My advice to you, Lady Everton, is to sail to France and never come back."

Cassie looked up in surprise.

The older man smiled kindly at her. "After seven years your husband will declare you dead, and you will be free to remarry if you wish."

Cassie lifted her chin and nodded stiffly. "Thank you, Mr. Penning. I am sorry to have wasted your time."

He nodded and stood to escort her to the door. "Good luck to you, Lady Everton."

She didn't bother to answer as she made her way out the door and down the street. Tears blurred her vision, and she blinked them away. Seven years was a long time. On the other hand, what else did she have to do? There was no other waiting in the wings.

Chapter Eighteen

Cassie huddled on the small bed as the ship pitched and rolled in the violent storm. She moaned, fighting the steady waves of nausea. In her grief she had not thought to procure more ginger root and the results of her forgetfulness was miserable. Her new maid was of little help since it turned out the girl was terrified of the sea. Cassie moaned again. She would rather be afraid than seasick. A chair crashed to the floor as the ship floundered on its side for a moment; then lurched back in the other direction. Squeezing her eyes shut, clutching the side of the bed, she wallowed in her misery.

"Cassie?"

She opened her eyes. Auggie stood in the doorway, feet braced against the bucking of the ship. "Why did you not let me die?"

He stumbled across to the bed. "Nay, lass, ye donna' want to die."

She closed her eyes as he sat down on the edge.

"What kin I get for ye?"

Cassie shook her head. "There is naught you can do for me, Auggie."

The ship pitched again and Cassie would have rolled onto the floor if Auggie hadn't caught her. She didn't protest as he wrapped his big arms around her and cradled her securely against his broad chest.

"I'm sorry lass."

"You cannot help the storm." Cassie sniffed.

A shudder rippled through his chest. It took her a moment to realize the man was shaking. Puzzled she squinted up at him in the dim light of the room. Something shiny glistened on his cheeks, and a drop of dampness fell onto her hand. *Was the great hulking man crying?*

"I'm so sorry, lassie. I tried to save 'em both, really I did."

Cassie wiggled against his chest in an attempt to sit up, but his arms held her captive, his body shaking with great sobs of grief. Before Cassie knew it, she was clutching him to her and sobbing as hard as he.

"I canna' claim to know how ye feel, lassie. I lost a good friend, but ye lost yer wee bairn and the man ye love."

The words hit Cassie as if wielded by a runaway coach and four. *The man she loved.* Her heart felt as if it were breaking at that moment. The tears she shed up till now were nothing compared to the grief which released itself in torrents in the comfort of Auggie's arms.

She clutched his shirt front as his lips brushed the top of her head; then turned her face up and looked into his eyes. The pain and anguish she saw there was like a mirror into her tortured soul. Her mind was in a fog when his lips locked onto hers, his kiss desperate, rough, and without meaning. She gave into his plea, wrapping her arms around his neck and returning his savage kiss with frantic thoughtlessness.

They shared their grief in this way until neither one could breath, their hands and lips roving, desperately searching for a release from the pain.

Auggie pulled away, his breathing ragged and his eyes wild. "Cassie, forgive me lass, for I dinna' mean to do this."

Cassie looked down, her breath coming in gasps as labored as his. Shame filled her. What was she doing? She wanted him, but not in the way she had wanted Cohen. This was a primal need, a searching for a release of all the pain, fright, and loneliness she carried for the last year and a half. *To give in to this feeling was wrong.* She pushed against his chest to free herself, but he held tight.

"I'm sorry, lass."

Cassie didn't need to look up to know the sincerity of his words. She stopped her struggles and leaned against his warmth. "Just hold me, Auggie, please. Just hold me."

They weathered the storm together, finding an odd peace in the sharing of their grief. By the time the sea calmed, the brutal pain was eased as well.

"Cassie?"

She rubbed her cheek, salty with dried tears against his soft tartan. "Yes, Auggie?"

"I promised Cohen I'd look after ye if any thin' happened to him."

Cassie smiled. "You have fulfilled your promise."

"Nay." He sat up and gently pushed her away. "I want to take ye to wife, Cassie. Marry me and I swear I'll protect and cherish ye for the rest of yer days.'"

If all her tears were not already spent she would have cried. "Oh, Auggie." She cradled his face in her small hands. "I cannot marry you, for I belong to Lord Everton for seven years. Until he is convinced of my death and has the marriage annulled, I will not be free of him."

Auggie nodded, but the determined look in his eye did not fade. "Then I'll wait. Until then, I'll keep ye safe and see ye are happy."

"Thank you." Cassie placed a light kiss on his cheek; then sobered, dropping her hands to her side. He wrapped his arms around her, leaning back so he was sitting up against the wall. Cassie took a deep cleansing breath and sagged against him. Her eyes felt heavy as he lightly stroked her hair. "I do not know what I would have done without you these past few days."

"I only wish I could have saved 'em for ye."

She closed her eyes, the soft rise and fall of his chest lulling her into a false sense of contentment. What was she going to do? She could not accept Auggie's proposal. It was not fair of her to make him wait, and did he not have a girl somewhere? Once they told Cohen's family where would she go? Perhaps she could find work keeping books somewhere. She yawned. It was not likely anyone would hire her when she did not even speak French very well. Perhaps she could ask Alex to continue to tutor her. *Now that I am alone in the world I will have to learn to fend for myself.*

"Auggie?"

"Yes lass?"

"Tell me about Cohen."

"He was a good man, and I am proud to 'ave called him my friend. We met on my first dig in Scotland. He was sweet on my sister Gwendolyn."

Cassie pushed aside the stab of jealousy at the thought of Cohen being sweet on anyone other than her.

"We always thought he'd marry her, but then the cave-in happened. Everton could not stand the idea of losin' out on a major find so he sabotaged the supports along the cliff. The side collapsed, my father and a couple others were killed. My sister thought Cohen was trapped down there, and she tried to go down herself to get him.

She fell from the cliff when the last support gave way."

She pondered his words. "Why did no one hold the earl accountable for his dirty deed?"

"Everton is a cunnin' bastard. We all knew he was behind it, but the men he hired mysteriously disappeared."

"Oh." Cassie yawned. "For what it is worth, I am sorry you lost your family."

His voice softened. "Thank ye, lass." He eased his bulk out from behind her. "Sleep now, lass."

She smiled as he tucked the covers up around her chin like a mother putting a child to bed. He did not love her and never would. All he wanted was to protect her; she could not let him throw away his own future because of his promise. No matter what, she had to make it on her own.

After Auggie left, she sat up and reached for the oriental box she kept by the bed. Her fingers stroked the top of the polished surface before she opened it and plucked out the little jade elephant. She rolled the smooth carving around in her fingers as was her habit when she needed to feel close to Cohen. The ship lurched and the box slid from her lap, clattering to the floor. She waited until the sea settled, and then leaned over the cot and picked up the box. A piece of the teak wood had broken loose and caught on the blanket. Gently she tugged it loose, the piece dropped into her lap along with a small velvet pouch. Setting the box beside her, she stared at the tiny black sack. Picking it up with trembling fingers, she untied the strings and dumped the contents into her palm. A piece of rolled up parchment paper fell out. She turned it around in her hands. An emerald encrusted ring held the paper in place.

Cassie slipped the paper from the ring and unrolled it, recognising Cohen's handwriting.

Cassie,
If anything should happen to me I hope you will find this ring. It is the ring I intend to place on your finger the day you and I are wed. Wear it and my family will honor my commitment to you and our son.
My love for eternity,
Cohen.

A single tear trickled down Cassie's cheek. When did Cohen hide the ring in her box? Why did he not tell her about the hidden compartment? She let the paper roll up and placed it in the box beside the elephant. Picking up the ring, she held it up to the small shaft of light filtering through the porthole. The emeralds flashed in the scant light, twinkling, the same color as Cohen and Lucca's eyes. She slipped the ring on her finger and settled back under the covers. Pressing her hand to her breast, she smiled. *He intended to marry me.*

Chapter Nineteen

Cassie shifted on the carriage seat, staring at the massive old castle looming in the distance against the churning seascape. *This was Cohen's home? No wonder his whole family lived with him.* The place looked like it could house an entire town with little difficulty. She glanced at Auggie. His leg twitched as his fingers worried the brim of the hat he held in his hands. *The poor man.* She could not imagine having to tell a family she was close to of their brother's death.

Auggie looked pained, his eyes blank and unreadable. The coach rattled through the weather whitened stone gates and up to the impressive matching steps. He set his lips into a grim line and opened the coach door as it came to a stop. After he stepped down, he turned, and held out his hand to her.

Cassie twisted the heavy ring on her finger. Would Cohen's family welcome her or would they see her as the instrument of his death? If she had anywhere else to go she would have fled at that moment, but Auggie needed her. Standing beside him was the least she could do to thank him for all his support. She stood and allowed Auggie to help her from the coach. He smiled sadly at her for a moment; then squeezed her hand. They were making their way up the steps when the door was flung open.

"Auggie!" A small dark haired woman squealed, making her way down the steps, leaning heavily on a cane.

He let go of Cassie's hand and hurried up the steps to intercept the woman, scooping her up in his arms and twirling her around. "Emmie, ye look ravishin' as always."

The pale woman giggled, throwing her arms around his neck and planting a kiss on his cheek. "You always know how to flatter a girl."

Auggie set her down with great care. "Only the pretty ones." He smiled and turned to Cassie. "Emmie, this is Cassie. Cassie, this is Miss Emily Ashton."

She caught her breath as Emily turned to her. Cohen's dazzling green eyes looked back at her from a feminine replica of his face. She blinked. "It is nice to meet you, Emily. Cohen has told me so much about you."

Emily blushed. "All of it good, I hope." She smiled. "How do you know my brother?"

Cassie drew a sharp breath. Auggie glanced at her quickly; then turned back to Emily.

"Emma, Cassie is Cohen's... She is the one he was gonna' marry."

"Fiancée?" Emily's brow furrowed and she tilted her head in puzzlement. "Where is my brother?" She looked past them at the coach.

Auggie took her hand and led her back up the stairs. "Where are yer sisters and brother? I wish to speak with ye all together."

Cassie followed them up the stairs and into the castle. Once inside Emily instructed the butler to take their wraps and summon the rest of her family. They followed as she led the way to a cozy family parlor. After they were seated, she rang for tea while they waited for the rest to arrive. The tea arrived in a timely matter as did the rest of Cohen's family. Cassie discovered Cohen's brother and three other sisters were carbon copies of himself. Five sets of his eyes stared at her curiously as she was introduced.

Auggie cleared his throat. "Devon, Penny, Clare, and Melissa, this is Cassie, Cohen's intended fiancée."

She fought back tears when Cohen's brother, as identical as if they were twins, kissed the back of her hand. The only difference between the two she could see was the light feathering of white hairs at his temple.

After introductions were made and everyone was seated, Auggie paced back and forth in front of the fireplace. "I have something to tell ye all. I guess I should start at the beginning."

Cassie looked down at the teacup in her hand as he began his tale. The cup rattled against the saucer, and she placed her other hand on the rim to steady it, trying to block out Auggie's words. This was the moment she dreaded. Would they hate her? Would they cast her from their house in anger? She could not blame them if they did; after all, she was a fallen woman and the indirect cause of their brother's death. Her subconscious registered their gasps and she steeled herself for their outrage. She looked up as Auggie finished the tale, and the women began to weep.

Tears rolled down Emily's face as she turned to look at Cassie. "Oh, Cassie! You poor dear, to lose my brother and your son must be heartbreaking."

Cassie blinked, astonished at the other woman's compassion.

Emily stood and hobbled across the room, enveloping Cassie in a fierce hug. "Never fear, you will stay with us and we will look after you." She pulled away, looking over her shoulder at her three sisters and brother. "Right, Devon?"

Cohen's brother wiped his misty eyes with his handkerchief and nodded. "Ashton's always take care of their own."

Her heart swelled at their compassion. Even in the midst of their own grief they opened their hearts to her as though she was truly part of their family.

The rest of the family came one by one and hugged her, and then Emily summoned the butler. "Perkins, please show Lady Everton to a guest room in the right wing. I am sure she would like to rest after her long journey."

Cassie stood and followed the butler from the room. The bedchamber she was shown surpassed even her wildest imaginings. The white stone walls were covered with rich tapestries depicting various medieval scenes that added color and warmth to the room. A footman was already lighting a fire in the large stone fireplace flanked by an upholstered armchair and settee. The bedchamber itself was a separate room. A large canopied bed covered in pillows took up the centre of the room, opposite it stood an oriental dressing screen, dressing table, and wardrobe. Tall glass doors led to a private balcony with the garden and the frothy sea beyond.

She wandered over to the glass doors and looked out. Bits of green already poked through last year's dried brown vegetation. The waves crashed against the jagged rocks, spraying vast fountains of spray and foam into the air. She leaned her head against the cool glass. *Where do I go from here?*

Her maid hurried into the room followed by a footman with the small trunk of clothes purchased in the little village of Lands End. "My lady, I will unpack right away. Is there anything I can get for you?"

Cassie smiled at the girl. She missed Sally. Not to say the new maid was not as good, but she did not seem to be at all interested in being friends. "No, thank you."

The girl looked at her solemnly. "The butler informs me dinner will be served at seven. I have taken the liberty of ordering you a bath."

Cassie nodded. *The girl never smiled.* She turned back to the view. It was probably for the best. A real lady did not fraternise with the help or so the earl often lectured.

The maid entered a small door opposite the bedchamber, and within moments, water gurgled into the tub. It seemed Cohen spared no expense in making the old castle as modern and comfortable as possible. Movement beyond the garden wall caught her attention. A lovely spotted deer wove its way along a narrow trail at the edge of the greenery where it met the sand of the beach. It paused, tail flicking, foot frozen in mid stride, and looked to where she stood. Even in her sorrow Cassie appreciated its grace and beauty. Its ears twitched before resuming its journey across the brown and green tufts of grass. She watched it until it disappeared from sight over a mound.

"My lady."

She turned from the window.

The maid gestured to the bathing room. "Your bath is ready."

Cassie followed her into the room. A large raised tub sat in the centre, the likes of which she had never seen before. The maid helped her undress; then she slipped into the deliciously warm jasmine-scented water. She leaned back with a sigh, enjoying the luxury of a hot bath denied her since before the night of the shipwreck. The sight of the deer and the soothing water eased her tortured heart and mind, bringing her to a place of calm acceptance. *God has exacted his punishment. There is nothing to do now but try to live a pious life and move on.*

An hour later she was bathed, dressed, and filled with a renewed sense of determination. She adjusted the hem on her simple, dark green velvet evening dress, and glanced up at the mirror. The color made her appear pasty and frail looking, but it was the only thing suitable for a mourning gown. At least the bodice was not as tight as her former dresses; no longer nursing, combined with her lack of appetite, had diminished the size of her breasts. A slightly tender ache made her press a hand to her chest.

A knock on the door made her turn. The maid opened it. Auggie stood on the threshold, dressed in a black dinner suit with a tartan wrapped across his chest. Cassie smiled. Even dressed in immaculate style the man still looked out of place.

He smiled back at her and shuffled his feet. "May I escort ye down to dinner, lassie?"

She nodded and took the arm he offered. They walked down the stairs to the dining room. Cassie hung back as they entered. It seemed like an entire village had come to dinner.

Emily hobbled forward to greet her. "Please, do not be put off by the size of our family." A small child darted between them, quickly scooped up by a nursemaid. "We all have dinner together, it is a chaotic affair, but Cohen would have it no other way." Her eyes saddened briefly, but a small quivering smile graced her lips.

Devon stood from his place at the head of the table and tapped his spoon against his wineglass. This seemed to be the cue for everyone to be seated as parents and children alike scrambled to their seats. Auggie pulled out a chair for her beside Emily. Once she was seated, he took the empty chair next to her.

Devon raised his glass. "Tonight, we welcome Cassie to our family." A baby gurgled and a chubby-faced toddler tossed his spoon to the floor with a clatter. Devon smiled. "I hope you will feel at home here, Cassie. I suppose proper introductions need to be made. You have met my sisters, Penny, Clare, Melissa, and Emily. Penny is married to William and those three delightful cherubs across from them are their children. Clare is married to Michael, the little darling who just threw his spoon and the baby next to him are their son and daughter. Finally, Melissa is married to Raoul, and those two wigglers there are their boys." He smiled at a pretty blonde girl beside him. "This is my new wife, Ann Marie."

Cassie nodded, overwhelmed by the introductions. One of the little girls giggled; then popped her thumb into her mouth. Her mother made an exasperated sound and pulled the appendage out.

Everyone raised their glasses as Devon finished his toast. "To Cohen, beloved brother and friend, we wish you a peaceful journey into heaven and to Cassie, we hope together we can help you heal and embrace life again." Everyone took a drink from their glasses, and then Devon returned to his seat. Serving girls passed around various dishes and the dining room returned to a controlled mayhem of voices.

Cassie placed a little bit of each food on her plate as it was passed to her. Somehow, a continent away she had stumbled upon a place that felt like home. She looked around the table. Mothers, fathers, and nursemaids worked together to tame unruly toddlers. Conversation flowed naturally with laughter and seriousness. *This is a family.*

"What are ye thinkin' lass?"

She smiled at Auggie. "I was just thinking this feels like…home."

He smiled back at her. "I thought it might, that's why I brought ye here." He glanced around the room. "I think ye will be safe and happy here while I'm gone."

"Gone? Where are you going?"

"I still have to commission a new ship, and there is still the dig in Sicily." He patted her hand. "Rest assured lass, I will be back, for I would not abandon ye when I 'ave made a promise to keep ye safe."

Cassie looked around the room. "I understand, Auggie. I think I shall be all right here."

Emily reached out and squeezed her hand. "Do not worry, the time will fly by. I am looking forward to your company, everyone else is always so busy with their family…." her voice trailed off, a remorseful look passing over her pale features. "I am sorry; I did not mean to be insensitive."

Cassie smiled at her. "It is all right, I understand what you mean. You and I can keep each other company." She was rewarded with a bright smile.

As the meal continued, Cassie relaxed and listened to snippets of conversation around her.

"Surely, Napoleon will come to his senses before an outbreak of war." Raoul said, shaking his fork for emphasis.

Devon shook his head. "Things will get bad between France and

England if he does not. His greed for power will cost this country dearly."

Clare looked up from spooning potatoes into her son's mouth. "Will we have to flee back to England if war is declared?"

Michael shook his head and placed a comforting hand on his wife. "No, dearest, we are French citizens through marriage and Cohen's title."

Clare looked relived and returned her attention to her son.

Cassie frowned. "What about me? If England and France go to war I will not be safe here."

All eyes turned to her. Devon looked thoughtful for a minute. "What say you, Auggie, since Cassie was not married to Cohen would she be in danger if she stayed?"

Auggie set down his fork. "I think it would be wise to keep her presence here a secret for now. If war were to break out, then perhaps we should consider havin' documentation forged to support a claim of French citizenship."

Cassie shook her head. "I cannot let you do that. If you were caught you would all be in danger."

"I'm sure ye will be safe until I return. If it appears ye are in danger I kin take ye with me to Sicily." Auggie patted her hand.

The talk at the table turned to Auggie's dig. Emily patted Cassie's hand. "Do not worry; you will be safe from Everton and Napoleon here."

The meal finished as nursemaids gathered the sleepy children and ushered them off to bed. The men headed off to the study for after dinner port and cigars. Emily linked her arm with Cassie's and led the way to the parlor; then sat at the piano and began to play a soft haunting melody. Clare handed Cassie a glass of dark liquid; she sipped and found the bitter almond and peach flavored beverage to her liking. Leaning back in her chair, she listened as the four women sang the sad tune in French. The final notes of the music faded away by the time the men joined them.

Devon hugged his wife as they sat together on the settee. "I think tonight, in honor of my brother; we shall devote the evening to fond remembrances of him."

Everyone raised their glasses. "To Cohen."

Chapter Twenty

Auggie inched his way along the hedge toward the back gate of Everton's mansion, pausing for a moment to listen. All was quiet except for the incessant chirping of crickets. He felt for the lock he was sure would be on the gate, but could find nothing. When he pushed on the iron clasp it swung open. He froze for a moment; aware the entry had been too easy.

A shadowy movement along the garden path caught his attention. Was it his imagination or was someone lurking in the dark? He drew his dagger, preferring its stealth compared to the noise of a pistol shot, and eased his bulk through the gap, cringing as his foot brushed a cluster of dried grass. The resulting tiny crackle sounded like a riotous boom in his mind. He slunk forward, his eyes trained on the spot where he had seen the mysterious shadow.

An arm closed around the column of his neck and squeezed. Before he could react, the click of a pistol being cocked against his temple warned him not to move. He froze.

A low voice whispered in his ear. "Drop the knife."

Auggie let the blade slip from his fingers. When he felt the stranger's grip relax he seized his opportunity. With a mighty heave he latched onto the arm and flipped his attacker over his shoulder. The man grunted as he landed on his back at Auggie's feet. Before he could scramble to his feet, Auggie leaped on him. They struggled, rolling around, each trying to gain the upper hand on the other. Finally Auggie got a hand free and aimed a punch at the other man's jaw.

"Bloody hell!" the man howled when the punch connected.

Auggie held back a second blow, his fist cocked in midair. *The voice sounds familiar.*

His hesitation was enough for the man to gain the upper hand. His fist struck Auggie's jaw. Auggie rolled to the side, his ears ringing from the force of the blow. "Ye addle-brained bastard!"

"Auggie?"

Auggie shook his head to clear the ringing and rolled to his feet, sure now of the voice. "Cohen? What the hell? I thought ye were dead!"

"Hush or we will both be dead!"

Auggie lowered his voice. "What happened to ye? I saw the cannonball hit where ye was standin'."

Cohen chuckled. "It did. The force of the blast shot me out over the water. The wind was knocked out of me, but I managed to crawl up onto a floating piece of debris. When I came to I heard the baby crying. By some miracle Lucca was floating a few feet away in his basket, damp and unharmed."

"Oh dear God! Cassie will be elated the wee bairn is alive."

"Cassie is alive?"

Auggie felt for his friend in the dark and squeezed his shoulder. "Aye, she is alive and well. I took her to Marseilles. She is safe there with yer family."

He heard the relief and emotion in Cohen's voice as he clapped his hand on Auggie's shoulder. "Thank you, my friend. I am forever in your debt."

Auggie choked back his elation. "What are ye doing here?"

"I came for vengeance."

"Me, too."

Both men laughed.

Auggie stood up. "What's yer plan?"

Cohen clambered to his feet. "I was going to break into his safe and steal everything of value the bastard has, you?"

Auggie clenched his teeth together. "I was gonna' kill him."

There was understanding in the silence stretching between them. Cohen's voice broke the quiet. "So what do we do now?"

Auggie thought quickly. "We scare the bastard straight. Come on."

They crept forward until they came to the veranda and paused to listen. All was quiet. Auggie waited as Cohen slipped up the steps and crouched down in front of the double doors. The house was silent, not a light glowed anywhere inside that he could tell. Auggie shifted impatiently. Finally his ears detected the tiny click of the lock as Cohen manipulated the tumblers to line up in order.

Cohen motioned him forward as he eased open the door. Together they made their way inside the earl's study. When Cohen crossed to the painting on the wall behind the desk, Auggie slunk to the study door. He opened it slowly and glanced both ways down the hallway beyond. There was no one in sight. He kept his vigil as Cohen lit a candle and worked to open the safe.

"Auggie."

He looked over his shoulder at Cohen.

"Come here and hold the bag."

Auggie took one last look out into the hall; then hurried over. He picked up the satchel and held it up as Cohen swung the door to the safe open. Inside, artifacts of different countries were stacked, along with jewels of many shapes and sizes. Auggie was not surprised to see the famed French "Tears of God" necklace, the elaborate piece consisting of thirty-one blood red rubies, reportedly stolen five years before from Napoleon's mistress.

Cohen removed piece after piece of stolen jewels and ill-gotten artifacts from their hiding place. Auggie noted he did not touch any of the money. Knowing Cohen like he did, the jewels and artifacts would be returned to those who lost them, for financial gain to the Emperor, of course. When the last piece was carefully placed in the satchel he closed the top. Cohen shut the safe and grinned.

The gas lights flickered to life. Both men spun toward the door. The earl and his butler stood framed in the doorway, the latter with a pistol pointed in their direction.

"I would say it is nice to see you again, Ashton, but I would be lying." The earl sneered.

Cohen's eyes flashed. "Why stop lying now, Everton?"

The earl's sneer grew broader. "You are awful cocksure of yourself for one who will soon be swinging from the hangman's noose."

"You are the one who will hang, Everton. All of the stolen jewels I just found in your safe prove beyond a doubt you are a thief."

The earl strolled into the room. "I have to hand it to you, Ashton, you are a first rate cracksman. Too bad you wanted to play above one's touch. I could have used a man like you."

Cohen's fists clenched, the muscles along his jaw twitching in irritation. "I may be of humble birth, but I draw the line at working for a lecher like you."

"A street rat with honor. How droll." The earl chuckled, hobbling forward and snatching the satchel from Auggie's hand. "Too bad your honor will not save you this time. Where is the girl and the child?"

"She is dead. You killed her just like you killed your last wife, Everton." Cohen's facial expression did not change.

The earl shrugged, not even pretending sorrow. "And the child?"

Cohen glared at him. "My son is hidden away where you will never get your vile hands on him."

Lord Everton shook his head. "You nick ninny, you did me a favor. Hand over your merry-be-gotten and I will let you go."

Cohen snorted. "Like hell you will, the moment you have your hands on the boy you will put a bullet in my head."

The earl looked over his shoulder. "Bernard, take these two down to the river. Kill them anyway you like, and leave their bodies for the fish."

Auggie peered at Cohen from the corner of his eye as Bernard motioned for them to exit the room. He picked up on the silent signal Cohen sent and walked ahead of him to the door. When he drew level with Bernard he reacted quickly, grabbing the barrel of the gun and wrenching it from the startled butler's hands. By the time he swung the weapon on the man, Cohen's arm was wrapped around the earl's neck.

"I believe if I were to feed your scrawny carcass to the fish they would spit you back out," Cohen growled with a triumphant look.

The butler looked back and forth between Auggie and Cohen.

"Do not do it," Auggie warned.

"Now, as I see it, Everton, you have a choice. You can give me the jewels and let us go on our way, or we can call the constables to sort all this out. I think they would be very interested in how you got all those stolen jewels."

The earl glared at Auggie, his eyes almost bulging from their sockets as Cohen tightened his grip. He wheezed and slowly nodded.

Cohen released him. The earl rubbed his neck and glared at him.

"If you *ever* set foot in England again, you son of a dockside whore, I will see you suffer an agonisingly slow death," the earl croaked.

"I have no reason to stay in England." Cohen reached for the satchel on the desk.

At the same time Bernard, drove his shoulder into Auggie knocking him off balance. Auggie tumbled backward as the gun went off. Out of the corner of his eye he saw the earl wield his cane at Cohen's head. He crashed to the floor, his attention shifting back to Bernard as they fought for control of the gun. The butler was a match for him in strength and size. They rolled back and forth along the floor, each trying to get purchase against the other.

Auggie glanced up in time to see the steel glint of the knife tip attached to the end of the earl's cane catch Cohen's arm. He heard the fabric rent and saw the blood quickly soak the dangling cloth of Cohen's coat. His face took on a pained look, mixed with anger, as he jumped back out of reach of the vicious blade. The earl swept the cane back across the top of the desk in an attempt to deliver another savage attack. This time it caught air; then the base of the candle on the desk. It toppled over, quickly igniting the papers on the top.

Auggie grunted and forced the barrel of the gun up under Bernard's chin as the flames grew, engulfing the drapes on the windows. Thick smoke billowed into the air as the flames licked their way up the wall to the ceiling. Breaking the butler's hold, he quickly flopped on top of the man, driving his fist into the butler's jaw he felt the bone crack as the man's eyes rolled into the back of his head. Panting and exhausted, Auggie pushed off the man. He looked toward the desk in time to see the earl slash at Cohen again. The tip of the blade left a bloody trail across his collarbone, and then impaled itself into the chair behind. The earl tried to jerk the blade free as Cohen stumbled around to the other side of the desk. Before he could loosen his weapon, the heavy iron rod holding the flaming curtains fell from its purchase on the wall, hitting the earl in the head. He crumpled to the ground, and his body was quickly consumed in flames.

Auggie lurched to his feet. "Cohen! Let's get out of here!"

Cohen shook his head. "We have to get them out of here," he yelled over the roar of the flames.

Grabbing the butler by the ankles, Auggie dragged him through the fire to the glass doors, kicked them open, and pulled the unconscious man out onto the veranda. He looked back, coughing and choking. *Where is Cohen?* A moment later Cohen stumbled through the door, dragging the earl's charred body behind him. He collapsed on the floor, gagging and coughing.

Auggie hurried to the earl. One look at the elderly man told him he was already dead. Lifeless eyes stared back at him from the blackened face. Auggie tossed his tartan over the smoking remains.

Fire bells clanged nearby. The blaze had been spotted and help was on the way. Servants hurried from the house and gathered on the lawn.

The butler moaned, and then coughed. He sat up and rubbed his jaw, his eyes widening as he took in the flames crawling along the outer wall. "His lordship!"

Auggie held the man as he sought to scramble back into the carnage. "It is too late, your lord is dead."

"What about the safe?" The man struggled, his eyes wild.

"The safe is made of iron, it should survive the fire." Auggie assured him. "Why?"

The butler bowed his head. "The earl's will is in there. He left everything to me. I served him for years, doing things I would rather not remember because he was going to leave everything to me. I ordered Ashton's ship sunk. I wanted to make sure Cassie and the child she was not supposed to have would not inherit what is mine."

Cohen fixed the servant with an incredulous stare. "You tried to kill us?"

The servant nodded. "The potion was supposed to keep her from getting with child."

Auggie grabbed the man by his shirt front. "What about my father and sister? Did ye cause their deaths, too?"

The butler shook his head. "Nay! I did not. I swear on my mother's grave, but I know the men who did."

The clanging bells grew louder as the fire waggons rolled onto the lawn. Fire boys jumped from the horse-drawn contraptions and began to work the hand pumps to spray the water.

The constables hurried forward. "What happened here?"

Auggie shoved the butler into his arms. "It is a long story best told over a bottle of port," he said with a grim shake of his head. He eyed the blood dripping from Cohen's arm. "And after my friend here gets some stitches."

Chapter Twenty-One

"Emmie, I really do not feel up to a social engagement yet." Cassie hurried from the milliners shop with Emily.

Emily smiled as the footman handed her up into the carriage. She waited until they were both seated and their packages stored before answering. "Nonsense, you cannot hide away in the house any longer. It has been two months since my brother's death. You have to get on with your life; you owe it to Cohen and Lucca."

Cassie sighed and looked out the window. "What about keeping a low profile?"

"Everyone believes you are Cohen's widow and, therefore, a French citizen."

"I just do not fit into the social scene, nor do I wish, too." Cassie glanced at Cohen's sister. "I never did."

"Come on, you know young Mr. Jacquie is quite smitten with you. You could do worse, you know. I hear he has a very promising up and coming career in politics."

Cassie shrugged. "I would rather die an old maid than marry again. Besides, I doubt Mr. Jacquie would wait seven years to marry me."

Emily sighed. "I suppose you are right." Her eyes brightened. "Why not? Auggie has been courting me for five years. He says he wants to earn his fortune before he asks Devon for my hand."

She bit her lip and looked out the window as the carriage topped the rise above the Ashton Castle. Poor Emily did not know of Auggie's promise to Cohen. It was time she struck out on her own. It would not do for her to allow him to marry her when Emily had been waiting all these years. Emily was her friend, the last thing she wanted to do was hurt the woman. As the carriage rolled down the incline and through the gates to the castle, Cassie made up her mind to leave.

"So? Will you come with us to the opera tonight?"

Cassie shook her head with a small smile. "Not tonight, perhaps next time, Emmie."

The carriage rolled to a stop and a footman rushed to help them down. Cassie headed to her room. She was relieved to find her maid not in attendance. Tossing her reticule on the dressing table, she crossed to the bed. The oriental box sat on the bedside table. She picked it up, flipping the lid open. Still inside was the sack of coins Auggie gave her before he left. There was more than enough to set her up in a small house and meet her needs until she found a job.

Tucking the money back into the box, she turned and pulled a large satchel from the wardrobe. One by one she packed her clothes, keepsakes, and accessories into it. By the time the maid showed up to help her dress for dinner, everything she wanted to take with her was packed and stowed away beneath the bed.

After she dressed, she made her way to the dining room. The room was in its usual uproar. Little William broke away from his nursemaid when he saw her and flung himself against her skirts, howling to be picked up. Cassie's heart pinched painfully, but she scooped Melissa's youngest child up into her arms. She cuddled him for a moment before she handed him back to the nursemaid. Would she ever get over the pain of cuddling another's child?

Melissa smiled at her, her eyes sad and apologetic.

They all pity me. Hiding her feelings, she took her seat. She would miss this, the noise, the camaraderie, but it was time to go. She sat through the meal, answering when she was questioned, but not volunteering any conversation of her own. When the time came for the ladies to retire to the parlor, she made her excuses and went to her room. She would wait until they left for the opera and make her way to the docks of Marseilles where she would find a ship to take her… somewhere.

It was well past dark when Cassie finally purchased passage on a mail coach bound for Bordeaux. Traveling by coach was preferable to braving the waves of seasickness that would surely result from a voyage by ship. After handing her satchel to the coachman, she climbed aboard. Gingerly she squeezed into the seat between an enormously fat lady of apparent gentle breeding and a low class man who reeked of gin. The man across from her gave her a sweaty nod.

She glanced at the other two beside him. The older man by the window was snoring softly and a young boy of about eight sat between the two. She smiled at the boy who stared at her solemnly. He blinked, and then turned his attention out the window as the coach lurched into motion. The drunken man flopped against her, his stale breath washing over her.

Gasping, she covered her nose with her handkerchief. *Perhaps the ship would have been better.* The coach raced through the darkness, leaving Cassie with little else to do but think or sleep; the latter being uncomfortable and not without risk. She shifted the drunken man toward the window and clutched her reticule. Auggie's money would enable her to rent decent lodgings for a month or two, in which time hopefully she could find a job.

She peeked at the young boy from under lowered lids. His eyes were closed and she couldn't tell if he was sleeping or not. The older man beside him shifted before opening his eyes. He stared at her for a moment and reached into the case at his feet, pulling out a napkin-wrapped package and a canteen. With a smile he folded back the linen to expose a couple of biscuits loaded with ham and cheese. He held out one to her with a friendly smile. When her stomach gurgled his smile widened into a grin.

Cassie reached for a sandwich. "Thank you, sir."

He nodded. "*Monsieur LeBonnet.*"

They ate in silence for a moment. When she was finished with her meal, he passed her his canteen. She drew the cork and tasted the sweet elderberry wine within. After a couple of sips, she handed it back with a smile of thanks.

He took a long drink, and then put the lid on and placed it back into the case at his feet. "My wife made the wine. It is good, *oui*?"

Cassie smiled and nodded.

He smiled again. "What are you doing out on your own at this time of night?"

"I am going to Bordeaux." She glanced around the coach, but the other occupants were fast asleep. "I am hoping to find a position there."

The man nodded as if he did not find a woman alone seeking employment at all unusual. "I am from Bordeaux. What kind of position are you looking for, *Mademoiselle*?"

"I have helped my father keep the books for the parish since I was old enough to read and write."

He nodded. "I see. As it happens, I am in need of a bookkeeper for my investing house."

Cassie regarded him through narrowed eyes. Was he a lecher, or did he, in fact, need someone to help as he proclaimed? He smiled again and handed her his card. She glanced at the header. He did own an investment company. She looked up and smiled at him.

"I can offer you thirty guineas a month."

"Thank you, *Monsieur*. I will gladly accept your offer." Cassie tucked the card in her reticule. Here she was, not a full day yet on her own, and she had already found employment. She closed her eyes. *I will be fine.*

* * * *

Cohen left his luggage at the docks and rented a horse to take him home. His eagerness to see Cassie made him too impatient to sit idle in a coach. He shifted the tartan he borrowed from Auggie that now held Lucca and leaned forward to urge the horse faster.

"Slow down, Cohen!"

He glanced over his shoulder at the Scotsman. The big man's horse struggled to keep pace with his. He tightened the reins and slowed his mount to an easy lope.

Auggie caught up. "The lass will still be there when ye get home." He grinned goodnaturedly.

Cohen cast him a sheepish smile. "I cannot wait for her to see Lucca, alive and well." He looked back up the road as his home came into view. They clattered along the cobblestone drive and up to the steps. Cohen leaped from the horse as soon as it stopped and tossed the reins to a startled gardener. He took the steps, two at a time.

"Cohen."

He paused with his hand on the knob and looked back at his friend.

Auggie pinned him with a solemn look. "Use caution, Cohen,

remember they all think yer dead."

Cohen nodded and opened the door. His footsteps echoed as he crossed the empty foyer. He stopped and looked around. Where was everyone? A door opened, voices drifting down the hall from the family parlor. He turned and headed down the corridor. He stepped across the parlor threshold and scanned the room. Emily sat on the settee, wringing her hands; Penny and Clare beside her, patting her shoulders. Devon and Raoul stood by the fire with their backs to him. The other women stood in the centre of the room, huddled in serious conversation.

There was never a dull moment in the Ashton household. He grinned and cleared his throat.

One by one, nine pairs of eyes focused on him, and then widened in disbelief. Emily turned paler, if that was possible; Penny and Clare gasped in unison and everyone else just stared.

He chuckled. "Is anyone going to welcome me home?"

Melissa let out a shriek and bolted into his arms. "Cohen? Oh, Cohen, is it really you?"

He wrapped his arms around her, careful not to squish Lucca as Devon and Raoul crossed the room and slapped him on the back. "Yes Mel, it is really me." He gently disengaged her arms as the others came to hug him.

Emily smiled and reached up to stroke his cheek as if to prove to herself he really was flesh and blood, not a ghost. "Auggie said you were dead." He smiled and placed a light kiss on the top of her head.

"I thought Auggie and Cassie were dead, too." Lucca let out a thin cry and Cohen lifted him carefully out of the makeshift sling. "As you can all see, I am very much alive. This is my son, Lucca."

Auggie entered the room and Emily threw herself into his arms. "Dear Auggie, you brought our Cohen back home to us."

Auggie's face turned red and he laughed. "We found each other."

Cohen smiled and hugged Devon. "Where is Cassie?"

The joyous tone of the room sobered. Devon dropped his gaze to the carpet, and Emily looked like she was about to cry.

Finally, Penny spoke. "She is gone, Cohen."

He stared at her in confusion. "Gone? What do you mean? Where did she go?"

Devon placed his hand on Cohen's shoulder. "I am sorry, brother, Cassie ran away last night."

"Why?" Cohen shook his head, trying to make sense of their words.

Emily sighed as tears rolled down her cheeks. "I guess she was ready to go. She thought you and Lucca were dead. I told her someone would wait for her if they really loved her like I have been waiting for Auggie. I guess she did not believe me."

Auggie groaned. "I told her I would wait until the earl declared her dead then I would marry her to keep my promise to Cohen." He glanced down at Emily. "I'm sorry, I should 'ave told ye. I only made the promise to ease her mind. I was sure she would find someone else before long. I suspect she left when she found out ye had feelings for me, Emmie. She would not 'ave wanted to steal me away and hurt ye."

"Where would she go?" Cohen looked down at Lucca, gurgling contentedly in his arms.

Penny took the baby from his arms as Devon squeezed his shoulder. "Raoul and I have scoured Marseilles, but there is no sign of her."

Cohen shook his head. "I was going to marry her. Everton is dead, she is free to marry..." his voice grew so thick with anguish that he could not continue.

Devon sighed. "We will find her little brother, I promise."

Chapter Twenty-Two

Cassie sighed and closed the ledger book. After rubbing her tired eyes she looked at the clock. *Another day done.* Pushing herself off the stool, she plucked her shawl from the chair and headed for the office in the back. She poked her head around the office door. "*Au revoir, Monsieur LeBonnet.*"

The older, fatherly man looked up from his legal book and smiled. "*Au revoir, Madame* Everton. Have a grand day off."

She took her usual route home along the boardwalk of the sleepy seaside town of Bordeaux. The baker waved to her as she passed and she waved back. *It is a nice town. Everyone is friendly and helpful.* She nodded to the cobbler's wife, Antoinette. She had been here for a little over six weeks, but yet she felt as if she had lived here all her life.

Young Basille Montonee stepped from his shop of fine silks and fell into step with her as was his habit of late. "*Bon soir, Mademoiselle* Everton."

"*Bon soir, Monsieur Montonee.*" Cassie glanced at him out of the corner of her eye. She did not have anything against the man, but his pursuit of her was wearing. She smiled sweetly at him. He pushed his spectacles further up his nose and smiled back. He was of average height and average build. His curly brown hair gave him a very young look. She could do worse, or so Antoinette said just the other day. *I am not looking for a husband.*

Basille smiled. "There is a *soiree* at *Monsieur Boigne's* tonight. I hoped you would come, *s'il vous plait.*"

Cassie frowned. "I am sorry, *Monsieur*, but as you can see by my dress I am still in mourning."

The young man shrugged. "Ah, *chere amie*, has it not been long enough to leave off your mourning? Long periods of grief are so *du vieux temps*, these days, *n'est-ce pas?*"

"*Tiens!* I was not aware mourning was so out of fashion these days," she said with a little ice tingeing her tone. When the man looked pained, she softened. "Perhaps I shall come for a little while, but do not expect me to dance."

Basille nodded and gave her a triumphant look. "*Merci beaucoup, Mademoiselle*. I shall come for you at eight o'clock."

Cassie nodded. Basille smiled, tipped his hat, and hurried back in the direction of his shop. She shook her head and turned the corner, hurrying up the steps to her rented lodgings.

A familiar voice called out to her. "Lady Everton?"

She swung around, her eyes settling on a young sailor crossing the street toward her. Wiping a hand across her eyes she looked again. *It could not be!* "Alex? What are you doing here?"

"My ship is docked 'ere for cargo. I saw you from ze deck." He smiled.

"I am happy to see you, Alex." He was definitely a sight for sore eyes. She missed his friendly banter.

Alex blushed and looked away briefly. "And I you, how is Auggie?"

Cassie folded her arms across her chest. "He is not with me. I am alone."

He looked puzzled for a moment, his brows knitting together. "Ah, well, I would be... pleazed to call on you, *oui*?"

"I would like that." She grinned.

Alex tipped his hat. "*Au revoir*."

"*Au revoir*, Alex," Cassie returned; then opened the door as he strolled away. She entered the small parlor and hung up her shawl. After kicking off her slippers she padded in her stocking feet into the small, but tidy, kitchen to put on a pot of tea. Already she was regretting accepting Basille's invitation for the evening. She filled the kettle and set it on top of the small stove. After a long day she certainly did not feel like dancing and making merry. Opening the stove door, she added a few pieces of coal to the meager glow to heat the water and warm the room. Summer would be here soon but there was a still a little spring nip in the air.

She stepped into the only other room in the house, the bedchamber, and looked at her reflection in the cracked mirror. A smudge of ink marred the bridge of her nose and wisps of hair framed her face where it had come out of her tidy braid. She better hustle if she was to be ready by eight.

The tea kettle whistled, and she hurried back to the kitchen. After pouring herself a cup of tea and spreading some preserves on a cold biscuit, she returned to her bedchamber. She flipped through her gowns as she munched, finally settling on a dark blue satin evening dress. Glancing at her waist in the mirror she frowned. Hopefully the dress would still fit without the usual corset underneath.

Popping the remaining piece of biscuit into her mouth, she headed back to the kitchen to heat up enough water for a sponge bath. The luxury of a bathing tub was something she desperately missed.

* * * *

Cassie finished tying her hair back with a silver ribbon and crossed the room to answer the knock at the door. She snatched her reticule up from the dressing table, donning her slippers as she went.

Basille stood on the other side, dressed in a fine suit of dark green broadcloth. He smiled and held out his arm.

Forcing a smile to her lips, she placed her hand on his arm. They left the little house and climbed into a rented coach for the short trip to the fancier houses of the merchant class. When they arrived at the small brick mansion, Cassie allowed Basille to help her from the coach and escort her up the steps into the modest ballroom.

Heads turned as they walked through the door and Cassie wondered briefly why she agreed to come. Many of the women whispered behind their fans, a few she knew already nodded. *They are probably wondering why such a pious widow, who spends all her free time in the church praying, would come to a social event.* She lifted her chin. *Who are they to judge me? Cohen would be proud to see I have grown a backbone since his death. No one is ever going to tell me what to do or how to feel again.*

Music began to play as Basille escorted her to a line of chairs placed along the far wall. "Can I get you a glass of punch?"

Cassie nodded; glad she spent all that time learning French from Alex. Her mind wandered back to their meeting on the steps of her house. It was nice to see him again. It was as if she could feel Cohen and Lucca when he talked to her. The familiar pain in her breast at the thought of Lucca returned. *Will the ache go away someday soon?*

Basille returned with the promised glass of punch. He handed it to her and sat beside her.

Sipping the tart drink, she watched the people as they mingled and danced. The pretty pastel colored gowns swirling and twirling mesmerised her, bright in contrast to her darker half-mourning one.

"*Mademoiselle?*"

She shook her head and looked at Basille. "I am sorry, you were saying?"

He patted her hand and smiled. "No need to apologise my dear. I wanted to talk to you. I have made no secret of my feelings for you, and I think you feel the same."

The smile on her face froze into a stiff mask. *Oh dear God. Is the silly little man going to ask me to marry him?*

He smiled. "Since there is no one else to ask, well, I wondered if you would permit me to court you." The look in his eyes was desperate, almost pleading.

She swallowed. Courting was the last thing on her mind right now. It was only three months since Cohen and Lucca were killed. Even if she was interested in the cloth merchant, she certainly could not consider a courtship at this time. "I am sorry, *Monsieur* Montonee, but I am not up to being courted just yet."

He looked crestfallen. "Surely it has been long enough to ease your grief? I swear I will court you with the utmost respect and reverence. I will give you everything you need, a fine house, silks, servants, and anything else your heart desires."

Cassie shook her head. "I am sorry, I am just not ready," she said with gentle force.

A half smile lifted the corner of his lip. "Then I shall wait until you are ready to accept my suit."

"Thank you for being so understanding."

He nodded, but his eyes took on a strange light. "Do not wait too long, *Mademoiselle* Cassandra, for I can be a very impatient man."

Cassie filed the comment away as a future warning with an

uneasy feeling.

Basille reached out and squeezed her hand, the strange look in his eye replaced with a sheepish grin. "I am sorry. I did not mean to speak to you in this way. Please, let me make it up to you."

"That is quite all right. I suppose I am just tired." Cassie withdrew her hand from his.

He nodded. "It must be hard on you to have to earn your own way."

Cassie nodded, looking away.

"Please, allow me to show you *Monsieur Boigne's* wonderful garden. He has quite an interesting collection of animals housed there." He stood and held out his hand.

Cassie's curiosity was roused. "What kind of animals?"

He smiled and winked. "Ah, a most impressive menagerie of African ones, I am told."

She hesitated. "I do not think it is appropriate to walk in the gardens unescorted."

"Ah, but all the couples here do, the walkway is lit so there is no danger of being out of sight of the main house."

She really would like to see the strange animals. The elephant on the dock had been very exciting. Perhaps there was one in the garden here she could view close up? She allowed him to help her to her feet. "All right."

Tucking her hand in the crook of his arm, he smiled and led the way out the double doors to the garden.

Cassie was relieved to discover the paths were indeed lit by lanterns hung every few paces. Basille led her to an assortment of large iron cages placed along the back wall of the garden. The first cage contained a funny looking brown animal. It swung back and forth from a perch in the cage by its long arms and tail. Cassie stepped closer and the animal let out a series of grunts and squeals. It sounded like it was cackling at her. "I have never seen anything like it," she breathed, fascinated. "It is almost like a furry little person."

She stepped away and wandered to the next cage. A large spotted cat looked back at her. His intense, yellow eyed gaze raised goose bumps on her arms. When he yawned, exposing a large set of fangs, she shivered and clutched Basille's hand. "He looks something like the statue the earl used to have from Egypt." She took a step back as the cat stood and stretched.

Basille laughed softly, "Does he scare you, Cassandra?"

Cassie nodded, uncomfortably aware of Basille's hands stroking her collarbone. When she opened her mouth to protest he pressed his clammy lips to hers, and then trailed sloppy kisses down the side of her neck. She tried to push him away, but he pinned her arms against her sides with one of his. He slipped his free hand into the top of her bodice.

"*Monsieur!*"

"Oh, how I want you, *ma cherie*." He groaned, his erection pressing against her thigh; then crushed his lips hard against hers in a bruising kiss.

Cassie whimpered and renewed her struggles as his fingers painfully pinched her breast. His strong cologne made her want to sneeze, his mushy lips and roving hands repulsed her. She did the only thing she could think of and sank her teeth into the soft flesh of his hand.

He swore and jerked his hand away, shoving her forward and kicking her legs out from under her at the same time. She fell, face first to the ground, gasping as the wind was knocked out of her. Before she could take action he flipped her over and pinned her down. "Let me go or else I shall scream!"

He smiled, the strange light in his eyes glinting with savage intent. "Go ahead, scream. Do you think anyone would believe your word over mine if I tell them you came on to me? I know who you are, Lady Everton." His voice grew cold and deadly calm. "Your husband is very much alive. You are hiding from him. Do you know he has offered a great amount of money for your return?"

"How do you know?" Cassie stared up at him, stunned.

"I have friends in high places in English government. All of London is a-buzz with the story of your 'kidnapping' and the theft of the earl's priceless artifacts. His reward would allow me to travel and hire someone to look after my shop." He sneered.

Cassie found her voice. "My husband would not be happy to have me returned to him ill-used."

"*Madame*, the reward was offered 'dead or alive.'" He snickered. "So, you see, if I take my sport with you first. It will not matter much to your husband."

She swallowed. "Please Basille, let me go. You have no idea how horrible a person the earl is. He probably will not honor his reward."

"I will take my chances." He shrugged. "The way I see it you have two choices, my dear. You can become my willing mistress, in such case if you please me I might be persuaded to release you at some point after I have tired of you, of course. Or, I can rape you as I please then return you alive or dead to the earl."

Cassie thought quickly. "What if Napoleon declares war on England? You will not be able to collect such a reward."

He shrugged again. "After I have my fill of you, perhaps Napoleon himself would delight in ransoming you to the earl. I am sure the Emperor would be most grateful to me."

Terror filled every fibre of her being. *I thought I could take care of myself. How foolish I have been.* What was she to do now? Perhaps she should convince Basille to turn her over to Napoleon. If she threw herself upon the Emperor's mercy may-hap he would let her go. If she showed him Cohen's ring, maybe she could convince him she was betrothed to him, if he didn't already know of Cohen's death.

"You are running out of time, my dear. I told you I am not a very patient man."

Cassie made up her mind in a split second as he lowered his face to hers to inflict another brutal kiss. Taking a deep breath she spit in his face and brought her knee up to connect with his groin. He let go of her with a startled howl, and she shoved against his chest with all her might, toppling him backward onto the grass. Scrambling to her feet she scanned the garden for a way of escape. If she ran back to the ballroom, everyone would ask questions she did not want to answer. Her eyes fixed on the back gate into the alley as Basille lurched to his feet. She jumped from his reach and bolted for the exit. *Please be unlocked.* Basille's footsteps pounded behind her. Was he gaining on her? She reached the gate and pulled on it. It swung open with a squeal of rusty hinges. She darted through the opening just as Basille grabbed the shoulder of her gown. The material rent with a loud rip but she jerked from his grasp, not caring her bodice sagged open, exposing most of her chest. Her slipper flew off as she ran, the awkward patter of the remaining shoe echoing along the dark alleyway.

She ran blindly down street after street, not knowing or caring where she was going as long as she left her tormentor behind. After darting around the corner of a building close to the docks, she paused and leaned against it, panting. She tried to quiet her breathing so she could hear if Basille still pursued her. *Are there footsteps behind me?* Unsure, she turned and ran down the street. She glanced over her shoulder, but did not see anyone behind her. As she turned her head back in the direction she was running, she collided with something solid.

Ooph! Her breath slammed from her chest as she stumbled and fell to the hard cobblestones.

"*Sacre blu!*" A man's voice uttered a garbled stream of French curses over her head.

Cassie winced in pain as she got to her feet. Her right knee ached and something warm and sticky trickled down her leg.

She brushed the dirt from her scraped palms and attempted to pull her bodice together. "I am so sorry, *Monsieur*."

"Lady Everton?"

Cassie jerked her gaze from the torn material. Alex stepped forward into the circle of light emitted from the gas street lamp above her head.

"Alex! You do not know how glad I am to see you."

He glanced down at her torn dress.

She crossed her arms over her tattered bodice. "A man, Basille Montonee, was chasing me. He…he tried to…to…he tried to hurt me." Cassie hiccoughed, tears weaving their way down her cheeks.

Alex took off his coat and wrapped it around her shoulders. "Come, I take you home, *oui?*"

Cassie nodded, and then looked back over her shoulder. The street was empty.

They turned the corner and Cassie paused, half afraid to see Basille there waiting for her. The street was abandoned. She limped along beside Alex as he strolled down the street to her rental, wincing as her shoeless foot was bruised by sharp stones.

Alex helped her up the steps and into the parlor. He lit the lantern and sat her on the worn settee. "I take look, *oui*?" He gestured to her knee.

She cleared her throat. "That is not necessary, I am fine. It is just a scratch."

Alex shook his head and disappeared into the kitchen. Cassie heard him pour water into the kettle and stoke up the fire. Within minutes he reappeared with a wash basin of warm water and a cloth. He knelt in front of her and slid her skirt up to expose her shredded stocking and bloodied knee. "I take care of you." He smiled and dipped the cloth into the water.

Chapter Twenty-Three

"I said no women on my expedition. I do not care if she is your sister; an archaeological dig is no place for a woman." The professor slammed his fist down on the scarred desk.

Cassie looked around the professor's study. It was well furnished with pieces from all over the world. Persian rugs, Chinese lanterns, and sandalwood accents, all boastful displays of a well traveled man. "I beg your pardon, *Monsieur*, but I could not help but notice your impressive collection of foreign goods." She smiled sweetly at the man when his eyes left Alex and swung her way. He looked her up and down like he was appraising a horse. "My former husband was a great collector of artifacts. It was my job to catalogue his amazing discoveries."

Interest sparked in the stern man's eyes as he pulled on his scruffy white beard. "What kind of artifacts, *Mademoiselle*?"

"His last find, before his death, was a very rare Egyptian cat. It was made of solid gold and had emeralds for eyes."

The captain's smoky grey eyes widened. "You do not say? Where did he find such a thing?"

Cassie licked her lip and smiled coyly at him. "I know a great many places my husband kept secret where such objects can be found."

His eyes narrowed as he contemplated her veiled innuendo. He arched one brow. "You would trade this information in exchange for passage with my crew?"

She nodded. "I could catalogue your many acquisitions as well, plus I can cook."

Alex nodded. "My sister is a fine cook, professor."

The professor heaved his rotund form from his chair and gave his trousers a yank, no doubt hoping to support his enormous belly. "Deal. Mind you keep confined to your personal coach when we travel. If there is any trouble, I will see you are tossed by the side of the road to fend for yourself, you hear?"

Cassie nodded, tossing Alex a triumphant look.

"Now scat, before I change my mind." The professor jerked his head toward the door.

Alex laughed as they made their way down the corridor to the worker's quarters. "I did not think the professor would say *oui*, until you told him you cook."

"With a belly like his I was pretty sure he liked to eat." She giggled.

Alex grinned and opened the last door on the right. "It is not much, but a least you do not have to share it with a bunch of terrible smelling men."

Cassie entered the room. Besides a mesh hammock there was a single three legged stool, a tarnished wash basin and a chamber pot. "It is better than waiting for Basille to turn me over to the earl." She gave Alex a false bright smile which she knew he would see through anyway.

He set down her small trunk of clothes and possessions. "I will come and get you in time for the evening meal. Do not unpack; we head out tomorrow before dawn." He squeezed her hand and left, shutting and locking the door behind him.

She sat on the stool. At least Alex would look out for her, and she would get to finally see what took place on an archaeological dig. Cohen had promised to explain the process to her one day. He promised to take her on a dig in Sicily. She wondered where Sicily was, and then realized she had not even asked where the professor's crew was going. Well, wherever they were headed, she would be away from the earl and get to see another land. It was an intriguing situation....

* * * *

A key scraped in the lock. Cassie steeled herself against the intruder as the door swung open, letting out a soft exclamation of relief when Alex smiled at her from the threshold. "Sorry to lock you in, but it is for your own good."

Cassie nodded. "I understand."

Alex gave her a grand bow and offered her his arm. "May I escort you to dinner, Lady Everton?"

She returned his smile and took his arm. "You know, 'tis not proper for a lady to have a male friend." When he looked down at her and frowned, worry lines etched in the corner of his eyes, she grinned and squeezed his arm, "but I am glad you are my friend, Alex."

"As am I, to have you as a friend, my lady."

They entered the museum dining hall. The room was crowded with men and even a couple of women, sitting, eating, and talking. A few looked up as they entered and gave her curious, but friendly, looks.

Alex led her to two empty seats and pulled one of the chairs out for her. She sat and looked down at the simple silver place setting in front of her.

"*Bonjour, Mademoiselle.*"

Cassie looked up into the kind eyes of a middle aged man.

He smiled. "I am Perrie Chanapelle."

Cassie looked at Alex.

"Perrie, is one of the dusting team."

She smiled. "I am pleased to meet you, Mr. Chanapelle. I am Cassie...Everton. What is a duster?"

"Please call me Perrie. Dusters are the people who sweep the dirt off any pottery, bones, or other artifacts that we find."

Alex leaned forward. "This is my sister's first time on a dig."

A servant came along and set a large pot of soup on the table in front of them. Alex ladled some into her bowl, and she smiled her thanks.

"Did you not take her with on any of your trips with Comté Ashton?" Perrie helped himself to a platter of biscuits.

Cassie's heart twisted at the mention of Cohen's name.

Alex shook his head. "She was married at the time to..." he looked at her quickly, "to an earl. Since her husband's death, she has been rattling around in that big empty mansion so I suggested she come along with me."

Perrie looked surprised, but if he doubted the story, he wisely refrained from saying so. "Pardon me, Lady Everton, for addressing you in an improper manner."

Cassie smiled. "No apology is necessary. Please, call me Cassie, the title belonged to my husband, not me. I am as common as you and Alex."

The young man smiled, and Cassie decided she liked him. He seemed genuine.

"So, Cassie, tell me how you managed to convince that nip cheese marplot, Professor Braun, to allow a woman on his expedition?"

"I complimented his collection, offered to catalogue his findings, and share a few of my husband's secrets."

He threw back his head and laughed; his rich baritone a welcome distraction. "You are a clever one, Cassie, to be sure. The only thing Braun likes better than crowing about his findings is eating."

Cassie laughed. "I did mention to him I can cook."

"You are a deep little minx." Perrie roared with laughter.

"Thank you." She turned her attention to her soup.

Perrie furrowed his brows. "You were not married to Earl Everton, by chance?"

She choked on her spoonful of soup. No matter where she hid, the earl would find her.

"I am sorry. Your husband's recent death must be still painful for you." He handed her his handkerchief.

Cassie patted her mouth with the clean linen. "Recent death?"

"I heard about the fire last month. Dreadful business it was. Is it true he left all his blunt to the butler?"

It was as if something slithered down her spine. She shuddered and swung her gaze to Alex as she fought to catch the breath that suddenly fled at Perrie's words. *Dead? The earl is dead? Am I finally free? Perhaps Perrie is mistaken.*

Alex reached over and took her hand. "My lady, are you all right?"

She looked back at Perrie. His gaze flickered back and forth between her and Alex, brows pinched together with concern. She fought to control her voice and look as if she knew the news all along. "You heard about the earl's... I mean my husband's death?"

He nodded.

Free at last. Alone. The words tumbled around in her befuddled mind. She hardly noticed Alex help her to her feet. The words he spoke to Perrie made no sense to her shocked senses. The room spun, everything blurred. She was vaguely aware of walking, the next thing she knew she was in her room. How she got there she could not fathom. Alex seated her on the stool. She recognised the concern in his eyes. "It is over," she whispered, almost afraid to say the words out loud. "He is dead. I am free."

He nodded and forced a glass of brandy to her lips. Where and when he had gotten it she could not recall. The first mouthful burned and she sputtered, but she downed the whole glass.

Alex set it on the floor as she leaned back against the wall, letting the soothing brandy take effect. "I am free, Alex. I do not have to run anymore. I can marry…." she let her voice trail off at the thought of Cohen. "I can marry if I wish to."

Alex brushed a tendril of hair from her forehead. "*Oui*."

She sat up. "I can go home Alex, home to my mama and papa."

"You will go?"

Cassie nodded. "I still have a little money left, enough perhaps to buy passage back to England."

He nodded. "You rest. I will see to your passage." He stood, kissed her hand, and left.

Cassie stared at the door as it closed behind him. *What will I tell my parents?*

Chapter Twenty-Four

Cohen shaded his eyes from the relentless Sicilian sun. It was only noon and already the heat on the hillside was almost unbearable. He swiped his arm across his forehead to wipe away the sweat trickling down, stinging his eyes. Another couple of hours and he would call a halt to the excavation for the day. Leaning back over the tablet, he returned to carefully sweeping the loose bits of debris from the exposed part of its surface.

Perhaps he should return to France. His heart just was not into the hunt for exotic treasures anymore. He missed Lucca. With a sigh, he dropped the brush into the dirt beside the relic and got to his feet. A local Sicilian boy wandered barefoot through the rows of workers, carrying a water pail. Cohen waved to him, and the boy hurried in his direction. He stopped in front of Cohen and looked up with a gap toothed smile. Cohen ruffled the boy's hair affectionately, reaching for the dipper hooked on the edge of the pail. He lifted it to his mouth, eagerly swallowing the fresh water. Once he drank his fill, he removed his hat and poured a ladle full over his head. The delicious coolness was refreshing.

He flipped the boy a coin and ruffled his hair again. The boy gave him a huge grin, mumbled something in his native tongue, and hurried away. Cohen smiled as the boy continued his rounds. Perhaps it was time to go home. His assistant could oversee the rest of the dig. His thoughts returned to his own son. Would Lucca be crawling or talking yet? Had he already missed those important first steps and words?

With little enthusiasm he surveyed the campsite below the hill. Militia exited his tent with her arms full of dirty shirts to wash. Even from here he could see the provocative sway of her lean brown hips under her flowered skirt. He tried to forget Cassie in the arms of the buxom dark haired beauty, but it had not worked. Like an untried school boy, his desire wilted and died before he even got her undressed.

Slapping at a fly buzzing a lazy circle around his head he realized he could not forget Cassie. He looked everywhere for her, but she had vanished like a drop of rain in a desert. Cohen shoved the hat back on his head and made his way down the hill. The dig had not brushed Cassie from his mind as he hoped it would.

He entered his tent and paused a moment to allow his eyes to adjust to the dimness. Tossing his hat on top of his clothes trunk, he wandered to the only chair and flopped into it. His restless gaze landed on the brandy decanter in the middle of the folding table, so he picked it up and poured himself a drink. He raised the glass to his lips and allowed the sweet fiery liquid to slide down his throat. The drink satisfied him in a way water could not. If he drank enough he could fall into a dreamless slumber, a muted sleep, where visions of Cassie's sensuous pale limbs and hair would not intrude.

Raised voices outside of his tent caught his attention. The men were excited about something when they spoke in that fevered pitch. Shadows of men flickered across the tent flap. What was going on? He stood and crossed to the entrance, flipping the flap open. Men were running from the campsite, down the dusty dirt road toward town.

Stepping from the tent he caught the arm of one of his workers. "What is going on?"

"The camp on the other side of the hill has had a cave in," the man said, shaking off his hand and following the others.

Cohen jogged along behind. When he crested the top of the hill, clouds of dust choked his throat and eyes. Holding his handkerchief over his mouth and nose, he scrambled down the embankment to the base of the other encampment.

He searched the chaos for the professor and found the man standing by the entrance to the collapsed cave, shouting orders, his white beard tinted red from the volcanic dirt. "Is there anyone in there?"

The professor nodded grimly. "Two of my men are trapped."

"What can my men and I do to help?" Cohen placed his hand on the man's shoulder.

"We need to shore up the entrance before we can try to dig them out."

Cohen turned and gestured to one of his men who had followed him. "You, go back to our dig and bring back all the unused supports you can find." When the man nodded and hurried back the way he had come, Cohen turned to the professor. Together they helped place the wooden beams brought to them into strategic positions around the opening to the cave.

An hour later the supports were in place, and the digging started. Cohen organised the men into shifts of four men, each digging until they were tired; then the next shift taking their place. It was almost dark when Cohen took his shift. He scraped the dirt with a trowel into a bucket until it was full, passed it to the man behind him and filled another. His muscles began to scream in protest by the time his trowel broke through the last barrier of debris. Tossing his tool to the ground, he signaled for the man behind him to pass forward a lantern.

He lit the wick, turned it up, and slid the glass back into place. With careful deliberation he eased his way through the narrow opening, coughing as handfuls of loose dirt slid from the top of the cave and showered down upon him. The dust swirled around the lantern, changing the yellow light to red. The results were shifting shadows that transformed the dark into eerie visions.

Cohen waited until the dust settled enough to see the sides of the cave, and then continued inching his way forward on his hands and knees. "Devilish scrape you have gotten yourselves into. Rattle on lads, so I might find you."

"Here, sir."

Cohen was relieved to hear an answer. "How many there?"

"Two of us sir, one hurt."

He kept creeping forward until the forms of two men took shape from the shadows. "What is your name?"

"Jacques, sir." The young man gestured to the man lying across his legs. "The other is Forchette."

Cohen held the light up with a start. "Alex?" Even in the murky light he was sure it was his former crew member. The man did not move or respond.

"Are you hurt, Jacques?"

"My arm, sir, it pains me."

Cohen pressed his lips together and thought for a moment. He held out the lantern. "Take the light and lead the way back to the entrance. I will follow behind with Alex."

The young man nodded, easing out from under his prone companion and took the lantern. As he crawled back in the direction of the cave's mouth, Cohen grasped Alex under his arms and dragged him along behind. The young man moaned.

"Alex?"

He coughed, "*Oui*."

"I will have you out of here soon."Cohen said a silent thanks the man was still alive.

"Comté Ashton?"

Cohen smiled at the disbelief in Alex's voice. "*Oui*." He looked behind, relieved to see the light from the entrance. A couple more feet and helping hands pulled the men from the tunnel. Cohen sprawled on the ground outside the entrance. Someone handed him a damp handkerchief and a canteen. He wiped the grit from his face and took a long drink to wash the dust from his throat.

"Comté?"

Cohen looked over at Alex who was being lifted onto a stretcher.

Alex stared at him. "Are you alive or have I died?"

Cohen chuckled and clasped the man's hand. "As you can feel, I am very much alive."

He let go of the man's hand as two men lifted the makeshift stretcher and headed to the physician's tent. The professor helped him to his feet. "A debt I owe to you, comté."

"Do you have anything stronger than brandy to drink at your camp?" Cohen smiled.

The man smiled back. "*Oui*."

Cohen clapped him on the back. "Good, share a bottle with me, and we will call it even."

"Ashton!"

Cohen turned around to see Auggie making his way toward him through the crowd. "Forton, you old devil! I did not know you were in Sicily."

Auggie clapped Cohen on the back and grinned. "It seems we are all after the same treasure, eh?"

Cohen nodded.

"Ye look like hell." Auggie frowned.

"Your waistline is the only thing that has changed my friend." Cohen grinned.

"Fudge," Auggie ran a hand over his protruding belly, "'Tis all the kick these days. The maids love a man who kin appreciate a fine table."

"I hope by maids you mean my sister." He winked.

Auggie sobered. "I came across a hellish sea to speak with ye on that, Ashton."

Cohen nodded, "Come on, we were just about to go have a drink."

They had just finished their second glass of rum when Cohen was summoned to the physician's tent. Auggie followed.

Alex lay on a cot in the corner, his head wrapped in a thick bandage. He waved Cohen over to his bed. "Comté Ashton, I must speak with you."

Cohen went to his side and laid a hand on his shoulder. "We can talk later, rest now."

Alex shook his head. "No, no. I must know what happened, how you are alive."

Cohen pulled a chair up beside the bed and straddled it, leaning his arms across the back. "There is not much to tell, I survived the shipwreck, drifted out to sea, and was finally picked up by a merchant ship."

"We all thought you were dead. Mr. Forton, he took Lady Everton back to your family in France—"

"I know. Unfortunately by the time I found out Cassie was alive and came looking for her, she was gone. I searched for her for months, but I could not find any trace of her—"

Alex waved his hand furiously to interrupt his explanation. "But Comté, I know where Lady Everton is."

"Where? Where is she?" Cohen stared at him, not believing his good fortune.

"She has gone home to England." Alex beamed.

Cohen frowned, his joy at finding Cassie floundering under the weight of their new predicament. "Now what am I to do?" He stood and paced back and forth beside the cot. "Napoleon has violated the peace treaty and declared war again on England." He shook his head. "Why did she not stay in Marseilles? If I sail to England under a French flag, my ship will be blown to pieces, and if I sail under a British Flag, I do not stand a chance of making the English coast line."

Auggie looked thoughtful. "Perhaps a Scottish vessel can make the journey."

Cohen shook his head. "England calls Scotland a friend, but you would not make it past Napoleon." He looked up as Alex cleared his throat.

"Perhaps, Comté Ashton, I may be able to offer a solution."

Cohen lifted an eyebrow enquiringly. "What say you?"

"Perhaps the solution is simpler than you think." Alex grinned; then flinched. He put his hand to his head. With a sheepish smile he continued, "What say we sail through Napoleon's army flying our French flag then hoist the British flag when within sight of England?"

Cohen sat down, leaned his arms across the back of the chair, resting his chin on his hand. He pondered the idea carefully. *Can I fool the British Army into thinking I am still a citizen of England? It just might work... Except for one thing.* He looked at Alex. "There is only one problem, how do I explain a French speaking crew?"

"It is simple, Comté, we teach the crew English."

Chapter Twenty-Five

"Mathew Lamb! Quit throwing rocks at Mary or I will fetch a willow switch!" Cassie stamped her foot to emphasize her threat.

Her little brother glanced over his shoulder at her, stuck out his tongue, and let fly another volley of gravel. His intended target, the baker's daughter, shrieked and ran for cover behind the water trough.

Cassie shook her fist. "I mean it, Mathew!"

Her brother scowled. "Make 'er go home then. Don't need no chuckle headed girl pesterin' me."

She groaned and tried another tactic. "If you do not stop, I will tell mama and she will make you recite bible verses all day."

William dropped his handful of stones and walked toward her, scuffing his worn boots through the dirt and bright fall leaves. He scowled at her with a ten-year-old's pouty defiance.

"Why not go with Mama to the Smith's? She could use some help carrying the basket of preserves."

William shrugged and headed off around the back of the church to their cozy living quarters.

Cassie shook her head and turned to re-enter the church. A gig bounced down the road toward her. She held up her hand, shading her eyes from the sun to see who it was, then groaned again when she recognised Penelope Stanhope's conveyance. Her hope of retreating into her former life was fraught with the barbed tongue of the vexatious young woman.

She sighed and headed for the church. She had notes to make for her father's sermon the next day. Her feet had touched the first step when the gig pulled up at the hitching rail.

"Oh, yoo-hoo, Lady Everton."

Cassie flinched but forced a smile to her lips as she turned around. "Good day, Miss Stanhope."

The groom helped the flamboyant woman down from the coach, and then stood at the horse's head. Penelope picked her way across to the steps as if afraid to get a spot of dirt on her pretty pink slippers that matched the sash on her white muslin gown and bonnet. "I so hoped to catch you at home."

Cassie tried not to cringe at the woman's sickly sweet demeanor. "Yes, well, where else would I be?"

Penelope giggled and carried on as if Cassie had not asked such a sarcastic question. "Mama says I should host a soirée to celebrate my betrothal to Squire Cumberland."

"What does your soirée have to do with me?" She glanced at the maid seated in the gig. The girl looked acceptably bored as she waited for her mistress.

The girl giggled again. "Well, mama says it would be a social *faux pas* not to invite you. After all, you are a Countess, albeit an impoverished one."

There, barb number one. Cassie rolled her eyes at the maid who cracked the smallest smile in response. How many more would she have to endure before Penelope went on her merry way? She turned back to Penelope and smiled sweetly. "Thank you for thinking of me, but I am afraid I must decline. Papa has not been well and he relies on me to help him these days."

Penelope returned her sweet smile with one of her own, but it did nothing to cover the ice in her gaze. "Really? I would have thought you would be spending most of your time praying these days."

Barb number two. Cassie crossed her arms over her chest, the smile fixed on her lips. "Why is that?"

Penelope blushed and tossed her perfect chestnut curls, her eyes widening in pretend surprise. "Why surely you have heard the rumors going around. It is just scandalous. I, of course, do not listen to rumors or gossip."

"Of course not, Penelope." *Barb number three.* Cassie bit her tongue to keep from saying what she really thought of the rumors she ran away with a traitor to the English crown; then was later cast aside by said man after the earl's death.

"Anyway," the girl continued, "I thought it would be especially nice of me to come and deliver the invitation to you personally." She held out a delicate scented envelope.

Cassie fought back the urge to tell Penelope how *nice* she thought the gesture was and took the envelope. "It was sweet of you to think of me. Now, if you will excuse me, I have a lot of work to do." She turned on her heel, shoved the invitation into her skirt pocket, and hurried up the steps.

She walked up the aisle between the pews, the same one she walked down the day of her marriage to the earl. *That day seems so far away. My whole life has changed.* Her thoughts wandered to Lucca. *How old would he be now if he were alive? Eight months? Would he be crawling, talking, or sitting up?* She shook her head. There was no sense in thinking about what might have been.

As she walked by the pulpit, she slowed, running her hand lovingly across its worn top. Papa would not deliver many more sermons from his mountaintop view of his flock. Everyday saw him weaker and more easily tired than the day before. A single tear trickled down her cheek. There was no money to look after her family when he was gone. The earl's promise was as hollow as his heart.

She sighed and continued on to the little room behind the chapel. The desk and chair sat where they had been since she could remember, right next to the little window so the light would illuminate the ledgers. Once again, she pondered her future. It was the same, yet different than last time. Beth no longer shared her bed, gone and married to a young minister from Dover. She was always the pious one, kind and loving to a fault. God favored the good and punished the wanton, like her. Like the last time she wondered what her future held, she was alone.

Flipping open the ledger on the desk, she sat. She had years to make up for her sins. Her eyes wandered down the columns, adding up the tithes for the month.

An hour later the books were tallied and in order. There was naught left to do but go over Papa's notes for the morrow's sermon.

"Cassandra?"

She paused and looked to the door where her mamma stood. "Yes, Mama?" Instinct told her something was wrong.

Her mother crossed the room and grasped her hand. Her fingers trembled, tears trickling down her face. "It is time," she said in a soft strangled voice. "Your Papa is asking for you."

Sorrow filled Cassie's heart. She had hoped for more time with her dear Papa. On unsteady legs she rose and numbly followed her mother. The others were there, the ones who still remained at home, her three younger brothers and two younger sisters. They watched her wide eyed and solemn as she followed their mother to the bedchamber.

Her father lay still against the pillows. His eyes were closed, his face slack and soft, like he was at peace with life and death. As she approached the bedside, he opened his eyes and smiled at her.

"My Cass," he whispered, his voice a mere shell of its usual bluster when he gave the words of wisdom from the Bible every Sunday.

Tears filled her eyes, and she struggled to keep them in check. Her voice broke. "Papa."

He squeezed her hand in his frail one with a surprisingly strong grip. "Do not cry for me, Cass, for I am ready to go and meet our Lord. He holds a special place for me in his lofty kingdom."

She nodded, not sure what to say and afraid if she did talk she would break down.

"You have been a good and dutiful daughter. I failed you, and for that I am sorry."

"Nay, Papa. It is I who failed you."

"No, I delivered you into evil as a sacrifice for the rest, and I shall have to answer to God. Tell me you forgive me before I die."

Sobs rent her body and she nodded, unable to speak.

Her Papa closed his eyes, gave one last sigh, and then slipped away into the forever after of passing.

* * * *

Cassie went through the days with quiet conviction. She ate when she had to, slept when her mind and body were too tired to do anything else, and mourned at her Papa's graveside like the rest of her family and friends. When word finally came of her father's replacement, she closed herself in the little study behind the chapel and cried.

Her mother found her there. "Cassie, do not cry so for this old house. It is only a place where one bids their time until the Lord calls

170

them home." She wrapped her arms around her, holding her close.

"I will miss the quiet solitude of this place. Where will we go? What will we do?" Cassie sniffled.

"The new clergyman will not be here for a few more sunsets. When he comes, we will go to the little cottage that was given to us in Dover."

"What cottage?"

Her mother smiled and patted her shoulder. "A man named Bernard came a few months ago. He said he owed you something for the suffering he caused. He would not tell me what or why, but he gave me the deed to the cottage and a large enough piece of land to grow what we need to survive."

Cassie shook her head in wonder. It seemed the earl's promise had been fulfilled despite his intentions and because of his death.

Chapter Twenty-Six

"Prepare to be boarded!" the cry rang across the water as the fleet of British frigates closed in on them.

Cohen glanced at Auggie and the ship's captain, decked out in their finest garb. Getting past the French had been the easy part, the English ships would be another story altogether.

The English frigate *HMS Victory* slid up alongside. Mooring ropes were thrown across and the boarding planks settled in place.

The vice admiral strolled across and stepped onto the deck, the pleasant smile on his face deceiving no one as he scanned the ship. Cohen plastered a like smile on his face and strolled forward to greet the officer. He suspected the Englishman's eyes missed very little, his relaxed posture a mere facade. This was a man who would be quick to anger, who would find the least excuse to sink them.

"I am Vice Admiral Nelson. Who are you and what is your purpose in English waters?"

Cohen exacted a polite bow. "Vice Admiral Nelson, is it? I have heard your great name brandied about in the highest social circles in London. Your exploits on behalf of England are legendary." He hoped the flattery would charm the admiral into relaxing his guard.

The admiral eyed him carefully. "Yes, we all do what we can for our country. You have not answered my question, sir."

He inclined his head briefly. "I am Cohen Ashton, sir, a humble cloth merchant on my way back to safer waters."

"I see." The admiral snapped his fingers and a dozen of his men spread out, searching the ship. "Did you run into any trouble from Napoleon's French swine?"

Cohen took care to keep his voice from betraying his disgust for the admiral's reference. "We did not, sir. For we sailed before the war broke out."

The admiral gave him a suspicious look. "If you left before the outbreak, then how is it you are still so far from an English port?"

"We were in Portugal, sir, aground for repairs." Cohen swallowed.

One of the admiral's men returned to his side and whispered something in his ear. The admiral dropped his hand to the handle of his sword at his waist. "How is it a cloth merchant has no bolts of material in his hold?"

This is the do or die moment. Cohen's hands shook. Either the admiral would accept his explanation, or they would be forced to fight for their lives. He glanced at Auggie and noted the tension in his jaw and the flex of his fingers above his own weapon. "Needless to say, sir, we were anxious to get back to London and did not complete our trade."

The admiral's hand tightened on his weapon and his eyes narrowed. "I see. I assume you have documentation to prove that you and your crew are English?"

A nervous sweat broke out on Cohen's forehead. Stealing artifacts was less risky than this venture was turning out to be. He reached into his pocket and pulled out a packet of papers and handed them over.

The admiral scanned the documents with careful deliberation before looking up. "These appear to be in order, what about that of your crew?"

Auggie stepped forward with the handful of forged documents they obtained for the crew. The admiral looked him over with interest and took the papers.

Sweat trickled down the back of Cohen's neck, but he stood unmoving as he waited. The tension stretched taut between his crew and the admiral's. He watched out of the corner of his eye as his men shifted restlessly and looked at each other.

The papers rustled in the breeze as the admiral shuffled through them. He looked up and fixed his gaze on Auggie. "You, there. Where is your documentation?"

Auggie handed over his paperwork.

The admiral glanced at it and raised his brow. "Scottish? Why are you on an English trading vessel?"

"Me ship was sunk by them French bastards. I and a few of me crew survived. We hopped a ride on this ship to get home to Scotland."

The admiral leaned forward and whispered something in his officer's ear. The young man turned and waved to the crew on the frigate.

This could not be good. Cohen took a step back as men began to file onto the ship. Every muscle in his body went on alert.

The admiral scanned the crew. "You there, come forward."

Cohen resisted the urge to look behind him and see who the admiral had singled out. If it was Alex, they would be all right. Alex spoke English so well now it was hard to detect even a hint of French accent. Cohen groaned inwardly as Jean Guiyesse stepped forward. If the admiral asked the sailor a question the man's thick accent would surely give him away.

Vice Admiral Nelson grinned, the lethal twinkle in his eyes telling Cohen he was calling their bluff. "What is your name?"

Jean looked uncertainly at Cohen; then back at the admiral. "Ju-ohn Smith, sir."

The admiral sneered, and then snapped his fingers. In an instant, thirty or more swords and pistols were pointed at them. "Tell your crew to drop their weapons, Ashton. You are under arrest for consorting with the enemy and treason to the crown."

Cohen signaled for the crew to drop their weapons, knowing it was useless to fight. The other two frigates in the vicinity made the chance of a victory against the British officer obsolete. His plan to get to Cassie had failed.

He did not offer any resistance when his hands were shackled in front of him, and he was led from the ship ahead of his French crew. As they crossed the narrow plank onto the English frigate, Cohen looked down at the sparkling water as it lapped against the side of the ship. *Cassie's eyes were the color of the waves.* He stepped down onto the opposite deck.

"Take the crew and the captain to the hold. Escort the Scotsman to my cabin and Ashton to the storeroom." Admiral Nelson turned on his heel and marched off down the deck.

Cohen smiled grimly at Auggie before he was elbowed ahead by an English sailor, across the deck and down a narrow set of steps to a storeroom. He was shoved into a cramped room and the door slammed shut. A key scraped in the lock, leaving him alone in the dark musty room.

Would they execute him or would they take him to Newgate to await trial? Would he have a chance to plead his case to the King? After all, he was still an English citizen. He sat down on the dirty floor. He would just have to wait and see.

Chapter Twenty-Seven

Cassie felt sorry for the old horse hitched to the little cart as she lifted the last of their worldly possessions out. The poor nag was long past her prime, but the best they could afford to get them to their new home.

Her mother waved from the doorway of the neat little farm cottage. "Cassandra, William says there is a buggy coming down the road through the orchard. I wonder if it is more livestock from Bernard?"

Cassie shaded her eyes and looked down the road. A small cloud of dust rose over the hill. With a sigh she handed the carpet bag to her little sister and grasped hold of the horse's bridle. "Come on, old nag. I will turn you out in the orchard to graze." She patted the sway backed mare and unbuckled her from the harness. The mare rubbed her head on Cassie's shoulder and snuffled softly in her ear. Cassie rubbed her between the eyes and led her down the road to the paddock.

A lone coach materialised out of the cloud of dust. She wondered absently who it could be as she flipped the latch open on the gate and led the horse into the paddock. She turned her back to the drive and slipped the bridle off the mare's head. After a final pat the mare wandered away, pawing away the thick carpet of leaves, nibbling here and there as she pleased on rare patches of still green grass. Cassie slung the bridle over her shoulder and turned around as the coach drew up beside her. She exited the gate, shut and latched it behind her, and looked up expectantly. The door to the coach was flung open, and a familiar face peered out at her.

"Sally? What are you doing here?" She dropped the bridle and ran to the coach as Sally climbed down. Cassie threw her arms around her old friend. They hugged each other close for a moment. Then Cassie stepped back.

Sally smiled. "I have a position as a ladies maid with Dowager Countess of Salisbury, who lives on the other side of town. Her young nice has come to stay with her, and her grace is looking for a companion of sorts to keep the girl company." Her eyes twinkled with mischief. "I heard you moved here and suggested you might be interested in the position."

Cassie gave her another quick hug. "You are a gem, Sally, and yes, I could really use the position. Mama has the farm, but she does not need an extra mouth to feed." She took the maid's hand and squeezed it. "Come on up to the house and meet Mama, and we can tell her about it."

"Only if you promise to tell me all that has happened since I last saw you. The earl was fit to be tied. He thought I had something to do with your disappearance and threatened to send me to Newgate until he found the grappling hook and his tablet missing."

They walked hand-in-hand to the house. "You would not believe it, Sally."

"I cannot wait to see the baby; he must be so big by now."

Cassie's breath caught in her throat and she struggled to say the words she must. "The baby died, Sally. He went down with Cohen and the ship."

Sally's eyes grew wide with disbelief; then clouded with sympathy. "I did not know. I am so sorry, Cassie."

"Come on, we have a lot of catching up to do."

* * * *

Later that evening Cassie was finishing up the last of the washing when her mother approached her. "Are you to go to the Dowager's on the morrow then?"

Cassie wiped her hands on her apron and nodded. "Oh, Mama. I am not sure I should. I never really fit in as a lady. People will whisper and gossip about the earl dying and leaving everything to the butler. They will think the worst of me."

Her mother patted her hand. "They might, but the true lady is the woman who holds her head up high and does what she must to survive."

"Yes, Mama." Cassie removed the apron and hung it on the peg by the fire.

Her mother smiled. "Perhaps you will meet a handsome young man who will ask for your hand. Then you will not have to stay here and look after your old mother for the rest of your life."

Cassie shook her head. "I do not want to ever marry again. I am happy here, looking after you."

"You are not happy, Cassandra. A mother knows when her child is heart sore. If I could but go back and undo all that has been done, I would." Her mother looked at her sadly.

She hugged her mother close. "I know, Mama, I know. It was my sin that caused my troubles, mine and mine alone. If I have to spend the rest of my life atoning for those sins, then so be it."

Her mother pulled away and took Cassie's face in her two hands. "Cassandra, I loved your father with all my heart, but I do not love the Bible as he did."

"What do you mean?" Cassie tilted her head. She always thought her mother was as pious as her father.

"I do not believe God is punishing you, just as I do not believe a soul is doomed to walk the coals in hell if they commit a wrong. I understand your love for the comté, even though your father did not, for I too once loved a man and lost him. My father, like yours, pledged my hand to a man I did not know. Soon after our marriage, I met a man who made my heart stir and my body sing. I was going to run away with my lover, but your father found out. My lover disappeared, I never saw him again and have no idea what happened. Nine months later, you were born." Tears sparkled in her eyes. "You deserve to be happy, Cassandra. One day you will find your true happiness again."

"Oh, Mama," Cassie cried flinging her arms around her. "How did you ever overcome the disgrace?"

Her mother's sigh ruffled Cassie's hair. "I devoted myself to your father, the church, and doing good. Soon people forgot all about it. Just as people will forget you were ever married to the earl. You will see, in time."

* * * *

Later that night, as Cassie lay down to sleep she pondered the story her mother told her. *Perhaps life is not just good and evil, light and dark.* Mayhap Cohen was right, she was not wrong to crave love and fulfilment. It was the earl's mistake for not wanting to love her. The sinking of the ship was not her punishment, but the earl's way of crushing a love he could not understand. Hell was not the place for someone like her, it was for someone like the earl, who was bitter and hate-filled. She rolled over and looked out the window at the stars twinkling in the heavens. Somewhere up there, Cohen cradled their son in his arms. She would see them again, one day. Until then, she had to take life in her hand and make of it what she could. Closing her eyes, she pictured Cohen cuddling their son and let sleep claim her.

"Cass, I am coming for you." Cohen smiled.

Her feet skipped across the deck of the ship. She had to get to him. He was her happily ever after. The deck seemed to melt beneath her feet; then she was falling, down, down, down.

Cohen floated above her with Lucca in his arms. "I am coming for you, wait for me."

Cassie bolted up in bed, cold sweat trickling down between her breasts and looked around. She was in her room, her trunks packed and waiting by the door for the coach to come and take her to the Dowager's. It was the same dream as every other night.

A movement out of the corner of her eye made her turn her head. "Cohen?"

The curtains fluttered gently in the light breeze from the half open window. With a sigh, she climbed from the bed and padded barefoot to it. She peered out into the dark. All was quiet. Nothing stirred. Grasping the shutters, she pulled them shut, latching them securely.

* * * *

Cassie smiled and curtsied to the Dowager Countess. "Lady Salisbury, I am pleased to meet you."

The dowager put her quizzing glass to her eye and scrutinised her.

"So, you are the former Countess Everton." She gave a muted *hrump,* and then dropped the glass back into her lap. "You, of course, will need to up date your wardrobe."

A flush of heat crept up Cassie's neck and she looked down at her black bombazine dress to hide her mortification. "Yes, Lady Salisbury. I have not had a chance to leave off my mourning as of yet, since I have been busy helping my mama."

The dowager nodded and gave her an approving look. "A good and pious girl observes the rules of polite society. After a trip to the *modiste* for some brighter half mourning clothes, I think you will do nicely. My niece, Charlotte, will be making her coming out in London this spring. However, since she has only her father and a nursemaid to instruct her, I thought it best she spend the winter here with me. It seems she has been her father's pet and has some rather…coltish ways about her needing to be tamed. You are, I trust, a very refined young lady since you were married to the late Earl Everton. Granted, he was a bit peculiar, I mean, really, hosting all male dinner parties? However, I suppose there is no accounting for taste."

Cassie bit her lip and looked down demurely. "Yes, Lady Salisbury."

"Now, on the subject of pay; you will receive a generous allowance, and I suppose you will need a maid?" She did not wait for Cassie to reply but continued on. "You may have my girl, Sally. She is much too young and silly for my tastes, mind you will have to share her with Charlotte. I have found a more mature maid I prefer."

Cassie nodded, trying to hold back her delighted smile.

"My butler will show you to your rooms. Dinner is at seven and my niece shall be arriving by the end of the week." She waved her hand in dismissal.

With a satisfied grin Cassie curtsied and followed the butler to her rooms. She could not wait to share her latest book by the new author, Sir Walter Scott, with Sally.

She was pleased to find her maid and friend waiting for her in her bedchamber. "Oh, Sally, this will be like old times. I even brought a couple of new books for us to read."

Sally laughed. "Oh good. I have really missed our reading

sessions. You are so lucky to have a father who thought it was a good idea to teach a girl to read. My father could not even write his own name."

Cassie squeezed her hand. "I have an idea. The Dowager's niece will not be here until the end of the week, how about I teach you to read?"

The maid's eyes brightened. "Would you? Oh, that would be grand," she breathed.

"We have a few hours until dinner, why not start now?"

Chapter Twenty-Eight

Cohen cocked his knee and dropped his arm across his eyes as he lay back on the musty smelling mattress. The clock tower clanged outside the tiny square window at the top of the wall. He counted the strikes. *One, two, three, four, five, six, seven, and eight. A guard should be making his rounds with the dinner trays soon. Not that the gruel is edible, but at least the bread is not too stale.*

The little stub of a candle he purchased from the guard for a ridiculous sum of one shilling flickered as an icy breeze slithered into the cell. He sneezed as dust swirled around the tiny room. The air had a crisp, damp feel to it, making him wonder if it was going to rain or perhaps even snow. *Did it matter?* He would be lucky if he saw the outside of these prison walls by spring, if ever again. It seemed the King did not take lightly English citizens in service to the Emperor, or having a French crew. Apparently the King had not heard—or had chosen to forget—he willingly turned over Everton's stash of stolen goods. He wondered how his crew fared. Were they, too, imprisoned here in Newgate, or had their fate been worse than his?

Shuffling footsteps and the jangle of keys announced the approach of the dinner guard. Cohen remained as he was, content to let the man leave his tray and go. A squeal of rusty hinges announced the opening of the door. He waited for the clink of the tray being set down and the door to shut. Instead, footsteps crossed to his bedside. Something poked him in the ribs.

Cohen dropped his arm. "If you think to torture me, get on with it already," he growled; then opened his eyes to scowl at his aggressor. The ample form towering over him in silence raised a hand, pushing the hood from his head. Cohen found himself staring into Auggie's grinning face. He swung his legs over the cot and jumped to his feet. "What are you doing here?"

"Hush. I've come to break ye out of this hellhole." Auggie tossed a priest's robe at Cohen. "Put this on, quickly."

"The gaoler will be around soon." He slipped the robe over his clothes.

Auggie chuckled softly. "Nay, he'll not be coming around for a while with the bump on the noggin' I gave him." He winked. "I hope ye do not mind, but I gave yer meal to the man in the next cell."

Cohen grimaced. "Mind? Hell, I would pay him to eat it." He snuffed the candle and followed Auggie to the door. They paused on the threshold, pulling their hoods up over their heads.

While Auggie relocked the cell door, Cohen slipped to the rail and looked down to the second story. Not a single guard was in sight. Together they jogged down the passageway to the stairs; then made their way to the first floor. Except for the sound of dripping water and a few noddy prisoners babbling incoherently, all else was quiet.

Auggie led the way along the corridor to the Chapel, ducking inside just as footsteps sounded on the far set of stairs. They pressed themselves against the wall, holding their breaths. The footsteps hurried past; then down toward the men's courtyard.

"Come on." Auggie motioned for Cohen to follow.

Cohen followed him back out into the corridor. "I hope you have a plan."

"Aye, a dirty one, but it'll 'ave to do." Auggie grinned over his shoulder and led the way to the closet at the far end of the cell bank.

They ducked into the closet and pulled the door shut. The stench was almost overpowering. Cohen watched as Auggie pried up the grate with an iron rod. He motioned for Cohen to help and together they lifted the square out of its cradle. Cohen looked down into the feces filled tunnel and groaned. "This is not how I envisioned my escape."

"What goes in must come out, so out we go," Auggie said, grinning from ear to ear. He lowered himself down into the tunnel until he dangled an inch above the flowing excrement and dropped. Cohen grimaced again as the foul sludge rose to Auggie's hips; then eased himself over the rim and into the hole. He let go, pinching his nose and plunging into the mire. The cold slime came as a shock as it rose to his waist.

Auggie grinned again and set off down the tunnel following the slow moving flow. Cohen shook his head and followed. If his siblings could see him now; he would be lucky to get the stink off himself before he reached France. Although, he supposed it was better than the alternative of swinging from the hangman's noose. He strained to see the Scotsman ahead of him in the murky tunnel. "I should have brought the candle."

"Did ye ever light yer bodily gases with a candle as a boy, Ashton?" Auggie chuckled.

Cohen snorted. "No, why?"

Auggie chortled gleefully. "'Tis better than gun powder, my friend."

Cohen groaned, catching his meaning. "It appears there is a great many things I do not know about you, Auggie." He shook his head as Auggie's snort of laughter drifted back to him.

They reached the end of the tunnel and found it blocked with a similar grate to the one in the closet. Auggie whistled long and low. A shadow appeared beyond the grate. After a moment a rope was passed through, and Auggie tied it to the bars. He whistled again and they waited. The rope tightened and the iron bars groaned under an unknown force. The rock around the grate began to crumble, and then it jerked free, landing with a splash in the canal beyond.

Alex appeared at the entrance to the gaping hole. "*Bon soir,* Comté."

"*Bon soir*, Alex." Cohen shook his hand.

Auggie lead the way out of the tunnel and swam across the polluted water of the canal, Cohen and Alex following. They pulled themselves out on the other side and hurried to the horses one of Auggie's crewmen held. They mounted and the four of them galloped from the outskirts of London.

Once sure they were not being pursued, they slowed their pace to a walk.

Cohen looked over at his friends. "I am forever in your debt, men."

Auggie grinned. "I will remember that and recall the favor if we get out of England with our heads intact."

"I hope we are going someplace with a bathing tub." Cohen grinned, wrinkling his nose at their terrible stench.

"Aye, if ye will settle for an icy stream and a bar of soap."

"It might take a couple bars to rid me of this terrible smell." His mount snorted and tossed its head as if in agreement. "See, even my horse is disgusted." Cohen's laughter mixed with that of the other men as they rode into the dark.

The sun was clearing the horizon when they turned onto a narrow path and followed it until they came to a small clearing where a bubbling brook flowed. After they dismounted, Auggie tossed Cohen a bar of soap and a towel from his saddle bags. "Yer an awful sight for these two eyes."

Cohen grinned and looked down at his dry, feces encrusted clothes. "You are one to talk. I hope you thought to bring me some clean clothes." He looked up as Auggie nodded. They stripped out of their clothes and waded into the water.

The icy water was a shock to Cohen's system. "Mother of God, it is cold!" As he scrubbed himself vigorously with the soap he looked over at the lone crew member who had not swam in the filth. "You best get a fire going or my manhood with suffer permanent damage," he jested. Everyone chortled, their spirits high with the successful completion of their mission.

Moments later, clean but shivering, they dried, dressed, and huddled around a roaring fire.

Cohen stared into the flames. "We are going to have to find a way to get through or around London to find Cassie."

"Nay, the lass is not at her father's parish."

Cohen jerked his gaze from the flames and stared at Auggie. "Then where is she?"

"I went to the parish. Her father died. Apparently they were given some land outside of Dover. She and the rest of her family left London a few weeks ago."

Cohen smiled. "Dover? Well, that makes things easier. It is only another day's ride from here."

Auggie cleared his throat. His voice was low and soft when he finally spoke. "Remember Cohen, she thinks ye are dead. It is possible she may 'ave married again."

Cohen sobered for a moment. He supposed it was possible. His heart ached at the very thought of his Cassie in the arms of another.

"First thing we do is eat then we will be on our way." Auggie rose, went to his saddle bags and pulled out some dried meat, cheese, and bread. He tossed them to Cohen along with a canteen and sat back down.

* * * *

They pushed their mounts hard, reaching the little seaside town of Dover just as the sun was setting. A few crisp flakes of snow drifted from the sky. Cohen looked up as they turned down the orchard lane they were told led to Widow Lamb's small farm. It was quickly clouding over. He hoped the snow would hold off a while longer. They would be pushing their luck to gain passage on a ship and make it back to France before the winter storms set in, if they could find a vessel willing to make the treacherous journey between the two countries. Perhaps it would be better to find a ship headed for Spain or Holstein Denmark and make their way across country to Marseilles.

As they approached the tidy little cottage a big, hairy sheep dog launched himself from his spot beside the door and loped toward them barking with fierce protectiveness. Their horses spooked and by the time they got them under control the widow herself stood at the doorway, musket in hand.

She looked back and forth between them with a worried frown. "What business do you have here?"

Cohen dismounted, passing his reins to Alex and held up his hands. "We mean no harm. We are simply looking for Cas-Lady Everton."

She swung the barrel of the gun toward his chest. "What do you want with my daughter?"

"I am Comté Cohen Ashton." He smiled when her eyes widened in recognition of his name.

Her look hardened. "What kind of devilish trick do you seek to play, sir? The comté died in a shipwreck months ago."

He gave her a slight bow. "I assure you, *Madame*, I am very much alive and well. The tales of my death are a mistake and nothing more."

She glanced past Cohen at the big Scotsman. "You there, you must be Auggie Forton, for I cannot picture any who fits the description better of the man my daughter claims saved her life."

Auggie nodded, dismounting and giving her a gallant bow. "Aye, I am, *Madame*."

She lowered the gun. "William, come take these horses to water," she called over her shoulder. A young boy of about eleven hurried from the cottage. He and Alex took the horses and led them around back.

Widow Lamb propped the gun against the door jam. "Please, come in while I set a pot of tea brewing."

Cohen and Auggie followed her into the cottage. They sat on the worn furniture in the cozy parlor. The Widow Lamb returned from the kitchen within moments with a chipped tea service. They waited politely as she poured.

Finally Cohen could stand it no longer and asked the question burning in his mind. "Where is Cassie?"

The widow looked up from pouring and set the pot down. She picked up her own cup and sat down across from them. "She is not here, your lordship. What do you want with my daughter?"

"I have come to take her back to France, to her son."

She gasped. "Lucca is alive?"

"Yes." He paused, uncertain he wanted to know her response to his next question. "Does she remain unmarried?"

"She is in service to the Dowager Salisbury, as a companion to her niece, but I beg of you to leave her be. Her heart has been hurt enough. Let her find what happiness she can, now after all the pain she has been through."

Cohen reached over and took her aged hand in his. "I have no intention of causing her grief. I must confess, I am a wanted man here in England. I have been charged with consorting with France and desertion of my country, but my intentions are honorable. I heard your husband is dead, *Madame*, I am sorry. The question that should have been asked of him I now ask of you. May I have your permission to marry Cassie?"

A small sad smile graced her lips, a single tear slipping from her eye. "Do you love her, comté?"

He nodded. "I love her and my son with all my heart and swear I shall protect them for the rest of my life, with my very life if need be." He handed her his wrinkled handkerchief.

She dabbed her eyes a moment before she looked up and smiled. "Then I give you my permission."

"Thank you." Cohen raised her hand to his lips and kissed it.

The widow looked over at Auggie. "Will you be going back to France with the comté?"

"Yes, *Madame*, for I, too, have decided to mend my wandering ways and marry his sister if he will give his permission."

She nodded, her eyes sparkling with emotion. "Then you will have to promise me you will watch over my daughter and her son if anything were to happen to the comté."

Auggie gave her a solemn look. "I swear to ye, *Madame*, I will look after them if anything happens, the same promise I made to Cohen the night the ship sank."

The widow nodded, apparently satisfied and returned her attention to Cohen. "You will find the Dowager Salisbury's home along the road overlooking the sea. Have a care how you find her, comté."

Cohen stood. "I will and thank you."

Chapter Twenty-Nine

Cassie sipped her glass of lemonade as Charlotte returned to the seat beside her, flushed and out of breath.

"Admiral Dickenson is a marvelous dancer."

"It is awfully hot in here," Cassie mumbled, waving her fan gently. "Are you ready to go home yet?"

Charlotte's eyes twinkled with excitement. "Oh, no, Cassie, it is far too early to retire. Aunt Whinny will not expect us home for hours yet. Perhaps a walk in the garden will cool you." She leaned over and whispered, "Besides, I happened to see that young officer over there watching you."

Cassie looked in the direction of the young officer she too noticed casting longing glances at her many times throughout the evening. He smiled at her before glancing away, a slight flush staining his clean shaven cheeks. "Really, Charlotte, I am not interested in being courted. It is too soon."

"But it has been months since your husband's death, and you are only in half mourning now."

"Come on. I think I am desperately in need of some fresh air." Cassie stood.

The two walked arm in arm out onto the veranda, down the steps to the wide garden path. They strolled along for a while, letting the cool breeze cool their heated flesh. Cassie pulled her shawl tighter around them as a few snowflakes drifted on the night air, her breath making ghostly clouds.

"Just think, Cassie, next spring we will be in London. I have never been to the city. I hear the balls there are so crowded one can hardly dance and one's dance card is full of men eager to find a match. Aunt Whinny says I should find a match quickly with my large dowry and good breeding."

Cassie smiled. "I am sure you will, Charlotte, you are very pretty." She cast an appraising look the petite raven-haired beauty. "Come on, let's go back inside. I am a little too cool now."

The two entered the ballroom. The young officer who had been watching her hurried over. He gave a polite bow. "I am Vice Admiral Sefton." His face flushed a deep shade of red. "I was wondering if, ah, you promised this dance to anyone?"

Cassie smiled at his lack of confidence. "No."

He grasped her hand in his and escorted her to the dance floor. Taking her in his arms gingerly, as if afraid she might crumble into dust, he picked up the rhythm of the orchestra. His gaze dropped to her shoes, face puckered in concentration as if wary he might step on her delicate dancing slippers.

She decided it was up to her to break the uncomfortable silence. "So, tell me Vice Admiral, how is it a man as young as yourself holds such an esteemed position?"

He glanced up at her. "My father is an admiral and petitioned the appointment for me. My older brother, Viscount Sefton, stands to inherit so I chose a career in the royal navy." He looked embarrassed and dropped his gaze again to her feet.

Cassie held back her sigh as his lips twitched, counting the steps and contented herself looking around the ballroom. She caught the eye of a couple of older ladies who glanced her way, whispering. They looked away and continued their unheard discussion behind their fans. No doubt they were talking about her. Did their husbands know the earl? If so, then it would not be long before they came calling on her to leach out information on her penniless state. *I feel a headache coming on.*

Thankfully, the dance ended, and the vice admiral escorted her back to her seat. Her head began to ache in earnest, and she wondered if she was coming down with a cold. When Charlotte returned to her seat Cassie gave her a pleading look. "Can we go home now, please? I have a dreadful headache."

"Oh, you poor dear. Very well, I suppose it is getting quite late."

They sent the butler for their wraps; then bundled up and climbed into their waiting carriage. Cassie leaned her head against the cool glass as the carriage made its way along the seaside road back to the Dowager's. Perhaps tomorrow she would ask the Dowager for permission to spend the day with her mother. The full moon peeked out from the clouds, the light reflecting the ridges of the restless ocean waves. It reminded her of her encounter with Cohen on the ship to Bath. The sea would always remind her of him. Clouds slid back across the moon, obscuring it once again from her sight. The only thing left to see outside the window was the shadow of the carriage and horses, illuminated by the coach's lanterns.

By the time they pulled up at the steps of the dowager's, Cassie's slight headache had bloomed into full blown pounding. She hurried up the steps to her room. The fire crackled in the hearth as Cassie entered her bedchamber and lit the gas lamp. She turned it down when it made her headache worse and summoned Sally to help her undress.

"You look tired." Sally favored her with a sympathetic smile.

Cassie rubbed her temples to ease the throbbing there. "I have a terrible headache."

Sally helped Cassie out of her Devonshire brown dress, on with her nightdress, and then brushed out her hair. "I asked the downstairs maid to bring you up a cup of chocolate."

"You are such a treasure. I do not know what I would do without you."

A tap on the door indicated her chocolate had arrived as promised. Cassie climbed into bed and smoothed the covers across her lap. She took the cup of warm chocolate and sipped it slowly.

Sally scooped up the discarded dress. "Is there anything else you need?"

"No, thank you, Sally. I am sure Charlotte is done talking to the Dowager and will be waiting for your help."

Sally nodded. "Rest well."

Cassie leaned back against her pillows. Already her headache was starting to ease. Perhaps reading would soothe her mind enough to sleep. She finished the chocolate, set the cup on the bedside table, and picked up the book she had been reading earlier that day. She opened it to the fourth chapter and made herself comfortable.

* * * *

Cassie yawned, glancing at the clock before she flipped the page. She had not realized it was so late. *Oh well, I will finish this chapter before turning out the light. Sally will see to it I sleep in.*

A tiny click caught her attention. Assuming it was Sally, she kept her focus on the page before her. "Please let me sleep in tomorrow, Sally."

When there was no answer she glanced up and gasped in surprise. A male figure shut the door, and then stepped forward into the light.

Cassie's heart pounded as she looked into Cohen's face. *It could not be. Perhaps I have fallen asleep without realizing it. I must be dreaming.* The book slid from her slack fingers and fell to the floor with a thud. She blinked at the intrusion of noise. The apparition stopped at the foot of her bed and smiled. *It looks so real. I can almost see the material of his shirt rise and fall as if he is breathing.*

"Cassie."

She scrambled back against the headboard, confused and terrified. *Did the ghost just speak? Am I finally losing my mind?* "Go away sweet featured ghost, for I have spent the last months vanquishing you from my dreams. Please do not seek to torture me during my waking hours."

He smiled and stepped around the corner of the bed.

"Nay! Keep back. Do not touch me with your deathlike fingers, for I am not ready to go there with you." She pressed herself harder against the head of the bed, her heart pounding against her ribcage.

"Cassie, I am not a ghost, nor am I a figment of your imaginings." He stopped at the side of the bed and reached for her.

She squeezed her eyes shut, afraid to see what he intended. The fingers that closed over hers were warm instead of cold. They gently caressed her hands like real flesh and blood. Unable to believe her senses, she peeked through her lashes. He smiled, the bed dipping beneath his weight as he perched on the edge. *It cannot be. He cannot be here. He is dead.*

"Cassie, my love, I am not dead." He took her hand and pressed it to his breast.

His heart beat there, a faint rhythm against her palm. She raised her gaze to his in disbelief. "How? How can this be? The explosion…

then you...were just...gone."

He smiled but kept her hand against his chest so she could feel the reassuring *pitter patter*. "We were adrift for more than a day before a merchant ship found us and pulled us aboard."

She reached up and felt his cheek. It was rough with a full day's growth of stubble, but warm. She did not bother to wipe away the tears flowing down her cheeks; instead she ran her hand along his face, remembering him with her fingertips. He was real, flesh and blood. *Perhaps it was a trick. Was this Devon in his stead?*

He let go of her hand, leaning toward her, his breath tickling her cheek and cradled her face in his hands; then drew her to him. His lips touched hers, his kiss tender and lazy. At that moment she knew it was him, no apparition or impostor could make her heart beat this way, and her limbs turned to liquid fire. His tongue begged for admittance to her mouth, and she opened for him. Groaning, he pulled her tight against him as he began his exploration. Her head swam as her heart fluttered like a million butterflies roosting within her chest.

A gasp made them pull apart and look to the door. Charlotte stood there, in her nightdress, her hand pressed to her lips.

"Hush, Charlotte, please, it is not what you think." Cassie scrambled from the bed.

Her eyes grew round. "You are kissing a stranger in your own bed in my aunt's home!"

Cassie hurried barefoot to her side and pulled her into the room. "Nay," she said, shutting the door behind her. "It is the comté, the father of my son. I thought he was dead, but it is not so. He has found me again. Oh, please, Charlotte, do not tell your aunt."

Cohen stood and gave a polite bow. "I am Comté Ashton. I have come to take Cassie home to France and her son."

Cassie spun around in stunned surprise. "Lucca is alive, too?"

He nodded.

Lucca is alive. She turned back to Charlotte. "Oh, please, Charlotte. My son is alive. Please do not tell your aunt. Let Cohen explain everything to her so you will not suffer any disgrace because of me."

Charlotte hesitated before she nodded.

Cohen stepped forward, taking Cassie's hands in his. "I am afraid we cannot tell anyone anything, for I have been accused of treason to the crown for having a French title and crew. Auggie broke me out of Newgate, and we must flee back to France. I have spoken to your mother, and she has given permission for us to marry. We must leave tonight, in secret."

Cassie nodded and looked to Charlotte.

The girl smiled. "How romantic! I will ring for Sally, and we will see what can be done."

Moments later Sally was ushered into the room. Her eyes grew huge when she saw Cohen there. "Merciful God, protect me from this ghost!" she shrieked.

Cassie clapped a hand over her mouth. "Hush, Sally. You will wake the whole house. It is really the comté, alive and well." When the maid nodded, Cassie lifted her hand.

The girl took a couple of cautious steps forward and felt Cohen's sleeve. Seemingly satisfied he was in fact real, she stepped back.

"Cohen has come for me. Lucca is alive. We are going back to France."

Sally glanced from one to the other. "How? You will never get past the British or French ships."

"I have found a merchant ship bound for Holstein. From there, we will cross over land into France." Cohen smiled.

"Come with us, Sally, please." Cassie squeezed her hand.

The maid shook her head. "It is too dangerous and I will not leave my mum."

Cassie nodded, understanding her friend's reluctance. "Then help me pack quickly, so we may be on our way before the sun rises and the rest of the house stirs."

Together the three of them packed a small bag of the essentials. When Cassie was dressed in a warm wool gown and cloak, Cohen opened the door and looked both ways in the hall beyond.

"Goodbye, dear friend." Cassie gave Sally a quick hug. "Thank you for your friendship when I was most in need of it. Take care of Charlotte now instead."

Sally nodded, tears coursing down her face.

Cassie took Cohen's hand and together they slipped out into the corridor. They made their way as quiet as possible down the stairs and across the foyer. The door opened as easily as they expected, proving most country homeowners did not keep their doors locked. They ran down the drive until they came to a stand of trees.

The big Scotsman stepped from the shadows, leading Cohen's horse.

"Auggie! How I have missed you."Cassie smiled, throwing her arms around the man.

He chuckled. "Careful lass, ye might make Cohen jealous enough to challenge me to a duel."

Cassie giggled, releasing him. Cohen helped her onto the horse, tied her bag on behind, and swung up behind her. Alex hurried from the shadows, leading two more mounts.

"Alex? What are you doing here?"

"Ah, *Mademoiselle*, I could not stay away, *oui?*"

Cohen nudged the horse into a canter and they fled to the docks.

Epilogue

Cassie rolled over in bed, gazing at the emerald ring on her finger, her heart bursting with happiness. The bed dipped as Cohen pulled her back against his warm chest.

"What are you thinking?" he murmured in her ear.

She smiled to herself. "I was just thinking how happy I am." She wriggled closer to him.

"Careful or you will be even happier in a moment, albeit late for breakfast," he teased.

She stretched leisurely with a carefree giggle. "Then let me up so I might dress."

"I like you naked." He wrapped his arms around her.

A sudden overwhelming sensation of sickness gripped her. "No really, Cohen, let me up, quick!"

He released her and sat up as she bolted for the bathing room. She knelt in front of the chamber pot and retched. When she finished she leaned against the wall and closed her eyes. His soft footfalls padded into the room. She opened her eyes. He held a towel and her dressing gown out. She took them, grasping his hand to help her up, the twinkle in his eye irritating her.

"Shall I send for some ginger root tea?"

She nodded, slipping her dressing gown on as he left. A few minutes after the maid finished helping her dress he returned, fully clothed, with the promised tea. He handed it to her as she sat at the dressing table, watching the maid fix her hair.

He caught her gaze in the mirror as she sipped and grinned, his eyes crinkling in that familiar way which made her think he found the world always amusing. "I hope this one is a girl, blonde and pretty like her mother. Perhaps I shall order a wardrobe full of pink satin gowns with little flowers along the bodice for her to remind me of the night I fell in love with her mother."

Cassie smiled. She would never forget that night as long as she lived.

Once the maid finished dressing her hair, Cassie and Cohen walked hand-in-hand down the stairs to the family dining room. The room was in its usual up roar. Cohen let go of her hand as their son toddled over to them on chubby legs with a lopsided grin.

Lucca held up his arms. "Pa-pa."

Cohen scooped him up and kissed his forehead. "Guess what, Lucca? You are going to have a baby sister or brother by next summer."

Emily leaped from her chair beside her new husband, Auggie, and hugged Cassie. "I am so happy for you. I cannot wait to have another baby around to play with."

Cassie laughed, looking around the room filled with men, women, and children. *This is a family.* She smiled at Cohen.

He returned it with one of his own, but his eyes smoldered with intense love and desire.

Guilty kisses turned into a love everlasting. This is the happiest day of all my nineteen years.

About the Author

Before being published I was a horse trainer, farrier, and riding coach. I have shown in everything from halter to show jumping. I currently reside on a southern Alberta commercial cattle ranch with my husband of sixteen years, my five school aged kids, and my thoroughbred stallion, Stamp de Gold aka "Love Monkey." Current projects include organizing Youth Writing Programs across Canada through MuseItUp Publishing and, as always, writing.

Also available at MuseItUp Publishing

The King of Silk
By Joe Douglas Trent
Historical Fiction
eBook ISBN: 978-1-926931-17-3

He heard himself groan and opened his eyes wide enough to observe a pair of spotless white sneakers planted on the curb inches in front of his face. In the gutter lay his magazine; his picture mocked him from the cover. A hand fished in his pockets.

Don't hurt me.

His mind replayed a photograph of an unshaven behemoth clad in a dirty orange ski cap and dingy athletic jacket despite the heat. The monster towered above him, pinning him with a crazy vacant stare.

Michael closed his eyes again and mumbled, "Just take what you want."

MuseItUp Publishing
Where the Muse entertains readers!
https://museituppublishing.com/bookstore2/
Visit our website for more books for your reading pleasure.

CPSIA information can be obtained at www.ICGtesting.com
Printed in the USA
237686LV00002B/24/P